What Aging Men Want

The Odyssey as a Parable of Male Aging

What Aging Men Want

The Odyssey as a Parable
of Male Aging

John C. Robinson, Ph.D., D.Min.

**PSYCHE
BOOKS**

Winchester, UK
Washington, USA

First published by Psyche Books, 2013
Psyche Books is an imprint of John Hunt Publishing Ltd., Laurel House, Station Approach,
Alresford, Hants, SO24 9JH, UK
office1@jhpbooks.net
www.johnhuntpublishing.com
www.psyche-books.com

For distributor details and how to order please visit the 'Ordering' section on our website.

ISBN: 978 1 78099 981 4

A CIP catalogue record for this book is available from the British Library.

Design: Stuart Davies

Printed and bound by CPI Group (UK) Ltd, Croydon, CR0 4YY

We operate a distinctive and ethical publishing philosophy in all
areas of our business, from our global network of authors to
production and worldwide distribution.

CONTENTS

Acknowledgements

This book grew from hours of rich conversation with forty amazing men - you know who you are! - who shared their lives with me, responded to my questions and ideas, and happily examined their aging experience through the images and metaphors of The Odyssey. I am deeply grateful to you and will be forever in your debt, though as friends, I know we don't worry about things like that.

Preface

Why I Wrote This Book

Stumbling through my seventh decade, I watched myself undergo a profound psychological, spiritual, and mystical evolution shared in my book *The Three Secrets of Aging*. It was a bumpy ride from unexpected and premature retirement into a new and expanded consciousness, but I also came to understand that we don't retire in enlightenment; the journey of aging asks us instead to find a brand new life in a world beyond retirement. In short, I needed to come home to my own place in the world. I also needed a guide to what this homecoming might entail.

My guide to male aging came from a most surprising source, *The Odyssey* – a mythological story reaching far back into the mists of time. *What Aging Men Want* draws on this powerful story to reveal the universal steps, stages, and thresholds that bring a man back from the war of adult life to his unique home in the world. Like Odysseus, I had been living on a beautiful island for seven years when the goddess, Athena, shape-shifting into my wife, said it was time to find that home. Then, as my own inner muse, she whispered *The Odyssey* and I knew instinctively this great story encrypted the guide I needed.

A sea voyage is a powerful metaphor for the journey home. Lest you think that coming home is easy, that you just relax and show up like nothing had changed in the past three or four decades, I assure you it is not. Rather, a man facing retirement and aging is again at the mercy of powerful and unexpected forces. There were times when I shook in terror, like Odysseus, as Poseidon, giant of the unconscious, roiled the emotional seas beneath my little ego raft; or felt as lonely and bereft as Odysseus missing my homeland despite living in paradise; or recoiled in horror at the wailing dead at the door of Hades as I faced the

I

possibility of a terminal illness. Images like these from *The Odyssey* are powerful because they reflect the complex and intense emotions embedded in the aging process. The many ways this myth parallels my own life are extraordinary and, given its ancient origins, may also be extraordinary for you too. I believe *The Odyssey* reveals the DNA of male aging and a prototype for man's possible elderhood.

A New Story for Men

Iron John, Robert Bly's seminal work on men at midlife published in 1990, sold over 400,000 hard copies, stayed on the New York Times Bestseller List for sixty-two weeks, and was translated into fifteen languages. More importantly, it ignited a men's movement that swept the nation touching an entire generation of men. I was part of that movement.

In men's gatherings across the country, Bly read chapters of his book to us before its publication, asking for feedback and testing his interpretations. His re-telling of this Grimm's fairy tale was spellbinding precisely because it was our own story – a story of midlife men searching for initiation into authentic manhood. Disenchanted with the traditional stereotype of the compulsive warrior, we needed a new vision. Interestingly, this new vision came from an ancient story symbolically revealing what men could be.

Bly's book, and the movement it stirred, changed me. I saw that psychology could engage the soul, not just the psyche, and that mythic symbolism was as true as any psychiatric formulation. From these realizations, I wrote my first book, *Death of A Hero, Birth of the Soul: Answering the Call of Midlife* (Robinson, 1995), endorsed by Robert and several other best-selling leaders of this movement.

Twenty years later, as I began to age, I found myself wondering what became of all those men initiated by the "wild man" in *Iron John*? Now in their sixties and beyond, where are they today and what are they experiencing? To answer that question, I interviewed forty men between the ages of 60 and 85, individually and in ongoing men's groups. In the process, I began sharing my fascination with *The Odyssey* as a parable of male aging to get their reactions. In time, I became convinced that every adventure Odysseus encounters on his voyage home to Ithaca symbolizes a developmental challenge all men face in aging. With this myth in hand, I sensed it was time to bring the men of *Iron John* home from the war of masculine life. It was time for a new men's movement – a movement of graying men surrendering their warrior armor for the mantles of elders, wisdom figures, mentors, lovers, artists and mystics.

Why write a book just for men? First, I know men deeply, starting with myself. I specialized in men's issues as a psychologist, ran men's groups for years, organized numerous men's gatherings, and wrote deeply about the male midlife journey in my first book. Second, as John Gray illustrated in his Mars-Venus books, men and women live different stories by virtue of their contrasting biological, psychological and social strivings. I want to speak to men about *their* struggles. Finally, because so many men have yet to find their own authentic voice and connection to self and soul in the aging process, I want to give them words and images to chart their journey. But while this is a book for men, it will also be valuable and accessible to women, providing insights about the struggles of the men they love and the masculine side of their own personalities.

If you are a man reading this book, I urge you to find your own life in the story. Find it in every page, every step of Odysseus' voyage home, and see what his adventures reveal about *you*. I predict you will discover new paths to meaning, unexpected insights about the life you have lived, and a kind of fulfillment in aging that you never thought possible. Your family, too, will better understand your experience of aging, feel less threatened by your changes, and begin to support you in a new way, for hidden in this allegory are many answers to the book's central question "What do aging men really want?" As we discover these answers together, you may also come to understand what *you* really want.

Questions for Men About Aging

Do you genuinely look forward to aging? Do you expect it to be filled with joy, creativity, love, new developmental tasks, and profound spiritual growth? Do you believe that aging and dying will reveal some of life's ultimate secrets? Or do you...

- View yourself as increasingly unproductive and useless now, lacking value, purpose, or position in the world or in your family?
- Compare yourself unfavorably with other men who seem more together and successful?
- Fear that time is running out and you haven't completed your "bucket list"?
- Dread aging as simply a process of inevitable physical and mental decline?
- Regret how you lived your life or feel ashamed of irrevocable mistakes?
- Feel embarrassed about these emotional struggles and keep them buried inside?
- Express your unhappiness indirectly through negativity, bitterness, or physical complaints?
- Keep busy to suppress your unhappiness or simply because you don't know what else to do?
- Use alcohol, marijuana, TV, travel, work, or hobbies to numb the dread and meaninglessness you feel about growing old?
- Joke about aging to hide or deny your real feelings ("It's better than the alternative, ha ha.")?
- Brag about how busy and happy you are in retirement

when your spouse or family might offer a rather different assessment (have you even asked them?)?

- Believe that aging is really just a period of waiting for death to rob you of everything that matters?

I have a dream that aging can be a radically new, fulfilling and joyful time saturated in love and generosity, quite literally the blossoming of your life. We've got aging all wrong and our culture's grim beliefs are "scaring us to death". Even our inevitable physical decline may be dissolution into an incredible new consciousness. But to experience this new consciousness, we need to come home, clean house, and wake up. Odysseus will show us how.

Introduction

The Odyssey: DNA of Aging Men

What Aging Men Want grew page by page from a deep and inspired reading of *The Odyssey*. An epic poem purportedly transcribed by the blind poet Homer over 2500 years ago, it tells the story of a famous Greek warrior coming home from a long and brutal war. First encountered by most of us in high school, it is a marvelous tale filled with full-throttle adventure, nearly unbearable pathos, and an explosive climax. It's a great read but what does this dusty old myth have to do with male aging?

The Odyssey and Male Aging

In the millennia before the written word and printing press, myths, fairy tales and fables were publically retold generation after generation, each dramatization gathering the feelings, experiences, and intuitions of the storyteller, his audience and his time. These stories were compelling and meaningful precisely because they embodied the essential themes, problems, and structure of the human psyche. From this archetypal ground, *The Odyssey* brings to life an ancient myth symbolizing our common and essential struggle with age. Because it enfolds thousands of years of experience, everything here is important – every detail, scene, action, conversation, emotion, and outcome. Revealing the symbolic DNA of aging men, this myth is the story of Everyman's final years. Its revelations will take your breath away.

The Odyssey presents a timeless allegory of what it means for a man to come home from "the war" of adult life. As we will see, from youth to old age, men engage in an all-encompassing drama of intense competition, heroic quests, and endless battles - a virtual war for status, power and love. Expressed in friendships, grades, sports, sex, career, income, children, and material wealth, this war not only permeates the journey of manhood, it defines it. Ask any guy to describe the battles he has fought, and still fights, to be successful and respected in his life, and he will have tales to tell about this war.

Put differently, in the last three thousand years, culture has changed, technology has changed, the world has changed, but the underlying biological and instinctual forces driving a man's personality have not changed. Every aspect of this story can be found around us today – in movies, novels, sports, business, religion, war, relationships, and everyday life. It has been said that "business is warfare in slow motion" and it is true. You think we have transcended our violent nature, think again. On February 2, 2012, a soccer match in Egypt between two top teams broke out in a brawl – 74 people were killed. It was "only" a game. Completing the story begun in *The Iliad* thousands of years ago, Homer painted a picture of masculinity and war that is every bit as pertinent today.

Though life spans were foreshortened by war, disease, and malnutrition in ancient Greece, *The Odyssey* nonetheless portrays the tasks aging men confront as they wind down their lives, surrendering long-practiced warrior valor and vanity, and coming home to an unfinished story of love and soul. We are called back to the tender and sentimental heart we put aside when the war years claimed us. The new aging – this unprecedented longevity now inviting millions of Baby Boomers into myriad untold possibilities, has made our return more obvious and important. As we understand this story's profound symbolism, we will understand the personal meaning and value of age at the deepest levels. Follow Odysseus home and you will discover his new and soulful life as your own.

Understanding the Odyssey as Myth and Cultural Dream

The Odyssey may be interpreted from numerous perspectives: mythological, psychological, philosophical, historical, literary, dramatic, or simply good entertainment. As a depth psychologist, minister, and aging male, however, I am most interested in the way it symbolizes the concluding journey of a man's life.

Depth psychologists have long urged us to find the myths we are living, for myths symbolically depict the unconscious dynamics of the psyche. Their universal themes inform novels, movies, politics, and the very meaning of life. It may be as simple as identifying with Dorothy on her imaginary trip to Oz where she eventually claimed – as we all must - her own intelligence (the scarecrow's brains), bravery (the lion's courage) and love (the tin woodsman's heart) in order to grow up. Aging, the other end of the life spectrum, also needs mythic tales to reveal its tasks and deeper significance. A story meant especially for aging men, *The Odyssey* provides that deeper meaning to guide a man home from the war.

How do we translate this story from an ancient poem to a modern parable of aging? Part of the answer dwells in under-standing mythic symbolism. Psychologically-oriented mytholo-gists view myths as symbolic expressions of the human mind, expressions that evolve as humans evolve. In particular, myths and fairy tales are said to represent humanity's collective growth of consciousness – of self, emotions, behavior, relationships, instinctual drives, developmental stages, and the nature of life. In summary, these ancient and colorful tales reflect symbolic attempts to understand ourselves by weaving stories about what we experience. The study of myths across cultures further reveals universal meanings for many symbols and for the journey the hero pursues across time and geography toward self-realization. As we understand these common motifs, we better understand both the people that created them and ourselves. I will bring this mythic consciousness to my interpretations of *The Odyssey*.

A complementary analysis of myths and fairy tales can also be uncovered with the skills of dream analysis. As mythologists and depth psychologists point out, dreams and myths come from the same unconscious recesses of the brain – the dream is an individ-ualized myth, the myth a collective dream. Both use metaphor, image, and symbol to *imply* meaning without needing to *explain it* with words, ideas and sentences. In essence, *The Odyssey* repre-sents a cultural dream about the nature of western man and his aging. Employing the skills of dream analysis, we likewise develop methods for understanding this great myth as our own story.

What are the skills of dream interpretation? To begin with, we understand that everything in a dream is symbolic – each image, figure, and action has personal psychological meaning for the dreamer and collective meaning for the culture. While dream figures can represent real people, they also represent parts of the dreamer. To decode a symbol's meaning, therefore, start by using the time-honored skills of *free association* and *imagination* that Freud left for us. For example, focusing on a symbol, let your thoughts and imagination wander freely without expectation or censorship, and see what comes to mind. Focus especially on details in the dream or story– the most fascinating, puzzling, or disturbing details – because they usually represent particularly important ways the unconscious is speaking directly about you or your life.

Another common interpretative technique is to assume that *every symbol reflects a part of you* (whether you like it or not!). So ask yourself if you were that symbol or image, what would you feel, think, or do? Similarly, have an imaginary *conversation with the symbol,* asking it questions, expressing your reactions, and seeing what unfolds. Write down this dialogue to record your discoveries. Another strategy asks you to *re-enter the dream* and explore it more fully as if it were still going on. Do something you didn't do the first time and see what happens. A related approach is to *dream the dream forward,* letting new things happen spontaneously in your imagination and watch where it goes.

It may also be helpful to *ask others to share their associations* to your dream. Ask them to finish the sentence, "If this were my dream…" and be fascinated by their associations. Since every symbol has multiple meanings, you will discover that the story's significance often varies or deepens as others reveal aspects of the symbols you hadn't considered. See if any of their associations trigger a new "aha" realization in you.

Once you have gathered information about your dream, turn it into a story with a beginning, middle and end. By making up this story, you will be converting the symbols and images into a fairy tale that the language side of your brain understands, allowing you to grasp its ultimate significance. Then look for parallels between your inner and outer lives. The most important discoveries are made when you can relate a dream's meaning to your ongoing life and its issues, problems, and challenges.

These techniques, which require practice to develop into real skills, will not only help you understand dreams, they will awaken amazing insights about *The Odyssey*. More importantly, they will help *personalize* my interpretations. As you get the gist of each adventure Odysseus experiences, use these tools of dream analysis to further reveal your own version of the tale. In this way, you will invite the story to reveal both its universal and personal significance. You have come to this myth to understand your life; Odysseus will not disappoint you.

The Book's Structure

For each step in Odysseus' journey home, I provide:

The Story. In a much-abridged form, I retell the story of Odysseus' journey home adventure by adventure, drawing out the most important symbolic elements of each chapter. As the story unfolds, keep in mind the larger context of this great and ancient tale. It is a metaphor of the challenges men encounter as they wend their way home from the battlefield of masculine life. Each challenge comprises a threshold of understanding – an experience that must be admitted to consciousness, understood and accepted for the journey to continue.

A Psychological Interpretation of the Story. After recounting each adventure in the story, I offer a general analysis of its meaning and significance drawn from my experience with mythological symbolism. Like archeologists, we will unearth a much more profound story beneath the surface drama, with the goal of going much deeper into the male psyche than those academic study guides you may recall from school. Your job then is to use the tools of dream analysis to bring out the story's personal meaning in your life. Have fun with it. You will be amazed by all you learn.

A Discussion of the Story's Relevance to Modern Men. To make this material additionally meaningful, I discuss how each section applies to actual men, men I have interviewed and know well, myself included, men representing our age and time. These were men who trusted me, men willing to share their personal lives. Compare their experiences and insights to your own aging and see what else you discover. While there are many paths through age, I believe the larger issues and challenges affect us all – we just work them out in our own ways.

A Summary of the Core Developmental Challenges. Each section of this universal tale offers a unique and powerful developmental challenge for aging men. I summarize these challenges so you can apply them directly to your own life, helping you further grasp what your own current problems mean and why your responses at each stage are so important. You can go deeper with the dream techniques we discussed, uncovering new insights into your own psyche.

Growth Questions. At the end of each section, I pose questions meant to help you further connect the story to your own journey. You might consider using a journal to record and deepen your discoveries. The first three questions apply my interpretations to your life; the fourth invites you to deepen the myth through dream work. Between the questions and the dream techniques, *The Odyssey* should speak directly to you.

Conclusions. After completing the symbolic decoding of this story, we explore two final topics: How we, as elders, can mentor each other on this common journey home and what aging men really want. Lastly, in the Appendices you will find instructions for forming your own older men's mentoring group and a powerful elder ritual that can be used with any man – you included – interested in consciously stepping across the threshold of age.

One Last Thought. This book strives to uncover the deep archetypal nature, purpose and course of mankind's third and greatest stage of psychological and spiritual growth – coming home. In timeless mythic symbolism, *The Odyssey* implicitly maps out the steps, stages, experiences, and challenges of this great adventure in human consciousness. At the most profound levels, we are seeking to reveal the structure and dynamics of an entirely new developmental stage. Reading *What Aging Men Want*, you become one of the pioneers of this amazing new era. I honor your courage and wisdom.

Chapter 1

The War Years

Our story really begins with the mythical Trojan War, a prolonged battle between two fierce and determined armies that dragged on for ten awful years. Described by Homer in his previous epic, *The Iliad*, this contest displays masculinity in its most vain, violent, and arrogant forms, and the reason for this war is so trivial and yet, in the world of men, so incendiary. I briefly summarize this background story because it is part of a larger human struggle we desperately need to understand and someday resolve.

The Story. *Zeus, the king of gods, has arranged a wedding high on Mt. Olympus between a goddess and a mortal. When Discord, another goddess, is excluded from this wedding (for obvious reasons!), she tosses a golden apple over the fence into the celebration inscribed with the words, "For the Fairest". A hand grenade would have been less explosive, for suddenly each goddess in attendance desperately wants this choice nickname. The field is finally reduced to three - Aphrodite, Hera, and Athena – and each claim the title. They ask Zeus to be the final judge. Wisely declining such a risky job, he refers them instead to Paris, a man known for his honesty.*

When Paris cannot reach a decision, the goddesses try their best to bribe him. Hera offers riches and power, Athena promises wisdom and military success, and Aphrodite bids the love of the most beautiful woman on Earth, Helen of Sparta. Paris chooses Helen, making Aphrodite the winner, and in the process makes enemies of Hera and Athena. Unfortunately Helen is already married to the king of Sparta, Menelaus, an inconvenient matter Aphrodite forgot to mention. Undiscouraged, Paris kidnaps Helen and brings her to Troy.

Menelaus is not the only one upset by this abduction. Because of

Helen's great beauty, Odysseus (whom we will meet very soon) had wisely advised Menelaus to require an oath from all competing suitors to support and defend the eventual winner of her hand. When Helen vanishes, Menelaus invokes this oath and soon Greece mobilizes for war. Paris' outrageous act also affronts the pride of all Greeks who now rally to avenge it.

The Iliad begins in the tenth year of the Trojan War, when conflict breaks out among the ranks of Greek military leaders. Their greatest warrior, Achilles, refuses to go on fighting. Once again, this turning point is based on a personal affront, for Agamemnon, the Greek commander-in-chief, has stolen Achilles' mistress. To make a long story short, Agamemnon eventually apologizes and Achilles returns to battle. Then, driven by enormous rage triggered by the murder of his best friend, Patroklos, Achilles exacts a many-fold revenge on the Trojan army, eventually killing and humiliating Hector, Troy's greatest warrior. In the end, the Greeks win. Ironically, Paris, who ignited this war, now strikes Achilles' heel with a divinely guided arrow, taking his life.

Interpretation. Like a long-running soap opera, *The Iliad* thrives on intrigue, surprise, cowardice, heroism, sex, violence, and hard-won lessons. Women compete in a rigged beauty contest, one man publicly humiliates another, a country inflames in patriotic fervor, war is declared, warriors compete for leadership and glory, and an Armageddon ensues taking thousands of lives in a seemingly endless bloodbath. What does this remind you of? Sounds a lot like the "modern" world to me (think: reality shows, political campaigns, business practices, professional sports, video games, block-buster action thrillers, porn, bar-room fights, endless wars…). It's so pervasive we take it for granted. Sex and aggression – Freud wasn't far off the mark.

The Iliad dramatizes the timeless and unfortunate fact that, despite our amazing intelligence, we men are still hardwired to be pack animals driven by deeply ingrained instincts to compete for the alpha male position (and the sexual dominance that comes with it). Add ego, money, power, and some awesome military weaponry, and the human species has become dangerous to all living things, and the Earth herself. Honor, glory, defeat, revenge, power, violence, secrecy, insult, war, revenge, honor – these recycling themes describe the same never-ending story of testosterone and ego. That Paris, who started this conflagration with his affront to Menelaus and the Greeks, takes the life of the nearly-immortal Achilles, Troy's greatest warrior, underscores the utter futility of this whole enterprise, and its irony – Achilles name is now primarily associated with his weakness.

But the thrill of battle is powerful for men – the sound and fury, power and ritual, spectacle and pageantry, suspense and adrenaline. It's intoxicating: hand-to-hand, body-to-body, man-to-man, in the trenches, fields, and airplanes, down and dirty, all-out, eardrum-busting bomb-exploding action. It's the heroism young men imagine, it's what they long for, it's who they are, it's what makes us men. In the end, this witch's brew of ego and instinct foments the endless clash of nations, civilizations and ideologies, of my god versus your god, my team versus your team, and the thrill and excitement of the next big contest. This opiate of powerful chemicals awash in male physiology is hypnotic, seductive, sexy, and addictive, infusing men with energy, purpose, and self-importance.

The Iliad, however, symbolizes more than actual warfare. It's about the battles men fight everyday at school, work, and in life. It's still war, only now sublimated in the workplace and driven by the invidious comparisons in income, status, power, appearance, wealth, achievement, cars, and women. This is the war of competitive masculinity; only in "civilized" society we kill each other with clever words and job-stealing manipulations. Has our nature really changed in the past twenty-five hundred years?

Discussion. You don't have to look hard for examples of this everyday war. Beyond the Super Bowl and Mixed Martial Arts, our aggressive behavior includes inner city gang members killing each other over perceived disrespect; CEO's demanding obscene bonuses while line workers barely make a living wage; workers at all levels competing for promotions and wages; stressful relationships with difficult bosses and scheming co-workers; politicians seeking election for ego, money, and power instead of service; and demagogues demeaning other nationalities, ethnic groups, or political positions for personal gain. Even in the most sophisticated settings – the university, the Vatican, the boardroom, the ruthless climb to the top infects everyone.

Every man has his own story of when he went to war, where this war took him, the wounds he sustained, and how he eventually stopped caring about winning. Men recall early war experiences in junior or senior high school – bullying, hazing, drinking, fighting, risk-taking, rule breaking, or chasing women – all to fit into the emerging social hierarchy. They remember the life-long game of comparison and competition over grades, athletic ability, clothes, looks, girls, cars, colleges, jobs, advancement, income and material wealth. Later they describe brutal bosses, competition for status, and salary on the job, and the awful reality that any time you "win" someone else had to "lose". Others, feeling they were losing in this game anyway, tried to become invisible or hid out in isolating non-competitive activities.

I remember being painfully puzzled in junior high as I watched elementary school friends regroup around the invisible new agenda of "coolness", swagger, and bravado. What happened to our old friendships? I remember the comparisons of high school – who were your friends, what were your grades, where were you going to college? When did I become a commodity? Then came the competition for graduate school admission, the need to impress faculty and peers, the competition for internships, jobs and success – I was running an endless gauntlet. By midlife, I felt exhausted and betrayed by the compromises I made to succeed. Like Odysseus, I longed to come home, I just didn't know how.

Can you identify this war in your life? If you're still working, how has it affected your work life? Do you push yourself on-the-job, tensing your body like a fist to enter the fray of bosses, problems, conflicts, meetings, phone calls, goals, obstacles, frustrations, failures, and decisions? Do you see others as enemies competing for the same limited spoils? When you're sufficiently cranked up, do you experience this tension as enlivening, fun, challenging – male hormones like drugs exciting new battles, goals and heroic adventures? Does it affect your friendships, limiting how much you like and trust co-workers or causing you to judge them with standards that make you feel superior by comparison or, just as often, inferior? If you're at the top of the heap, do you secretly feel like a conqueror? Or do you feel more like a soldier fighting together with comrades in the same unit? If you are retired, do you feel even worse now that you have nothing to show for yourself – no job title, income, power, or status?

It's a matter of age. High on testosterone, young men experience this war montage as exciting, adventurous, and challenging as they compete for valor and glory. As the middle years drag on, we may try to become inured to it, seeking comfort in lower expectations at work or the emotional bonds of family - if we have found a safe and pleasant haven. Later in life, we often find ourselves growing weary of this endless battle, believe we will never reach our original goals, and dream more and more of retirement, freedom, and peace. Hormone levels drop, physical strength declines, senses weaken, and older bodies no longer feel the same aggressive energies. In this context of increasing vulnerability and declining warrior ambition, aging men long to come home from the war.

At its highest levels, *The Odyssey* describes mankind's journey home from the universal male battleground symbolically depicted in *The Iliad* to the wisdom of age. It is a story of man's long slow struggle to achieve a mature awareness of self, world, and divinity, and a story of western culture's slow transition from a war-based value system to the enlightened consciousness of the immanent divine as the world itself. This cultural myth, depicting our transformation from violent animals to enlightened elders, is a gift from the collective unconscious that asks us to understand ourselves and save the world before it is too late.

The Challenge: Understanding the Male Psyche. With incredible intelligence and highly refined killing powers, we humans are gods with pack animal instincts. We war with each other just as the mythical Greek gods did, crazed by glory, power, jealousy, and revenge. Yes, there are more noble motives available – love, family, generosity, creativity, soul, and service – but most of us, when threatened or provoked, fall back instantly on our 10,000 year-old penchant for warfare. Can this hardwiring be changed or is it the very essence of our humanity without which we would not be human? We will carry this great riddle with us as we move forward and see what *The Odyssey* has to tell us in the end.

Growth Questions

1 Describe your own life-long experience of male warfare. What were your victories? Who did you defeat and who defeated you? What warrior behaviors are you most proud of? Least proud of?
2 Where were you wounded most deeply? How do you still carry this wound? What re-opens it?
3 When did you grow tired of the battle? Has it been difficult for you to give up the war and come home? If so, how?
4 Step back into this story as if it were your own dream.

What detail draws your attention? For example, what do you see at Zeus' wedding? What do you think of these goddesses? Which bribe would you take? Does your choice also lead to war? What is your "Achilles Heel"?

Chapter 2

Longing for Home

Every workday for thirty, forty, or even fifty years, we go off to war – at the office, factory, clinic, business, or farm. Every day we put on our armor, tense up, leave home and family, do things we don't always enjoy (sometimes forgetting what we once did enjoy), and fight the good fight, often coming home too tired to share much of what happened that day. We soldier steadily across the never-ending landscape of war, with its heady peaks of victory and valleys of failure and despair. While good times with the kids, vacations, home improvement projects, hobbies and dreams keep us going, they do not end the war.

In the daily grind of the compulsive warrior, distance grows between spouses, between father and children, between ego and soul. Our partner gets tired of asking how things were today and the children know better than to bother Dad when he's stressed out. In the early years, we still communicate about our lives, hopes, and dreams. Ten years later, the dust storm of daily demands and pressures obscures real sharing; twenty years later, everyone is too busy, distracted, or numb to ask; thirty years later, the kids have left to pursue their own wars, and our marriage can sometimes feel distant or mute. When was the last time you talked together about how you really feel about your life, your relationship, or your dreams? Do you even know how you really feel? Do you know how your partner feels? Is there too much water under the bridge to even ask?

As men weary of war, as it loses its meaning and luster, we begin to long for home. We search our daily experience for something long gone – feelings of happiness, hope, and love. Where are they now? We remember the early days when meaning and purpose inspired our lives. Where is that inspiration now?

We may feel lost, unmotivated, alone, even depressed. For some, this dilemma seems like a huge and fathomless problem; for others a background hum of boredom, doubt, and discouragement. But for most men in their late sixties, status and responsibility have morphed into chains. Moreover, we often find ourselves tangled up in relationship problems that we did not see developing, or did not want to see – buried hurts, disappointments, and power struggles that increasingly smother communication.

The weary heart now searches the horizon for home, but where is home and how do we get there? I carried this poignant question with me for years even after formally leaving the war. The family of my childhood and adult years had changed so dramatically – there was no going back to it. The old work no longer called to me and I could not bring myself to settle for the customary volunteer activities as a solution. I longed for something I couldn't identify and sensed that this longing would not be resolved simply – it was going to require a major transformational journey.

Odysseus, too, struggles valiantly with this question, his struggles symbolized in each of the amazing adventures he encounters on his journey home. Like all of us, Odysseus abandons love in the pursuit of ego – the essence of war! – and the painful physical distance separating him from his wife, son, and homeland symbolizes this estrangement of heart. As we accompany Odysseus on his journey home, we will understand the tasks and stages of aging, and perhaps find our own way home as well. But this journey of healing and understanding will take time – it took Odysseus ten years. It took me ten years as well. We must be patient with matters of the heart and remember that the symbolism of homecoming is best understood in the language of our own lives. And because the collective psyche does not yet understand this new phase of life, we must be its pioneers.

Come with me now into the magical life and times of Odysseus traveling home from the war. By the end of this tale, you will discover that he is you.

The Story. The Odyssey *begins with the goddess Calypso holding Odysseus captive on her island. He fell in love with this beautiful sea nymph on his journey home and she promised him immortality if he would be her husband. After several years of apparent happiness, however, Odysseus begins to ache painfully for his wife and homeland. He is tired, sad, and homesick. Homer tells us that the gods ordained his homecoming, but it was Athena, Zeus' daughter, concerned about Odysseus' growing depression, who finally begs her father to set him free.*

We also learn that nearly twenty years earlier, Odysseus left his wife, son, and palace on the island of Ithaca to join the Trojan War. In his absence, Odysseus' palace was taken over by haughty suitors scheming to win the hand of his wife, Penelope, and take possession of his kingdom. These powerful men loiter in the castle, squander his wealth, and arrogantly impose on his staff. Odysseus' son, Telemachus, still a callow youth, cannot stand up to these men, who mock and belittle his authority.

Because the war has been over for years, everyone assumes Odysseus perished on his way back to Ithaca. Penelope, hoping against hope that her husband will miraculously return – but increasingly strangled by the suitors' tightening noose – promises to choose a new husband as soon as she finishes a shroud she is weaving for Odysseus' father, Laertes, who has retired in old age to his orchards and vineyards. Every night Penelope secretly unweaves the shroud to delay this fateful decision.

Beginning the action, the goddess Athena, disguised as a man, secretly advises Odysseus' son, Telemachus, to go in search of Odysseus. Telemachus angrily announces to the Assembly of Ithaca that he is leaving to find his father. Athena then disguises herself as Odysseus' aged friend, Mentor, the man he asked long ago to look after

his son and castle, in order to secure a ship for his journey. She shape-
shifts again into the image of Telemachus to hire a crew. When the ship
is loaded, Athena evokes a strong wind and joins Telemachus on his
voyage.

Telemachus first seeks counsel from his father's oldest friend, the
loquacious King Nestor, who recalls traveling with Odysseus after the
Trojan War but says that they parted ways before arriving home.
Nestor in turn refers Telemachus to Menelaus, the husband of Helen
whose abduction began the Trojan War, who is in the midst of a great
feast celebrating the weddings of his son and daughter. Menelaus
recalls hearing that Odysseus was indeed alive and being held on some
distant island. Back in Ithaca, the suitors plot to ambush and murder
Telemachus, who has become a nuisance and an obstacle to their plans.
By now, Penelope is nearly overcome with grief and desperation, so
Athena sends her a reassuring dream that her son is alive and safe.

Interpretation. Before reading my interpretation, explore your
own associations to this beginning. Play with the symbols and
images, converse with a character in the story, discuss it with
friends, let your imagination enrich the story, and make it your
own. Does anything in this opening remind you of your own
life? The more connections you can make, the more the story will
grab you, and carry you into its action. Then see how the interpretation deepens this journey within. Again, go slowly –
wisdom is not gained through speed.

As the story opens, each member of Odysseus' long-divided
family grieves for their continuing separation. Husband longs
for wife, wife for husband, son for father, father for son. It is the
poignant call of family and love that stirs a man's heart to come
home from the war, and the gods ordain that it should be so. This
is the archetypal fountain of longing that swells up as a man
ages. Countless forays into the masculine world of heroic quests
and epic battles have absorbed more of his life than he ever
expected; he has ignored his family and his own heart for too

long. Painfully out of balance, his soul aches to come home to love.

Who are the suitors dominating Odysseus' wife and home, and how are they part of a man's aging? Keeping in mind that each figure in a dream or myth is part of our own psyche, we can hypothesize that the suitors represent personal ambitions, competitive struggles, greedy schemes, and warrior fantasies still active inside. By middle age, the psyche is overrun with them as we put aside intimacy, love, and even family for multiple all-consuming warrior projects. Sooner or later, our capacity to love – our feminine side symbolized by Penelope – is held hostage by these multiplying ambitions that now occupy and control the kingdom of our psyche. Like much of western civilization, our motives have become corrupt, greedy, and selfish, and the wisdom of mature authority is tragically absent or frankly disre-spected.

Athena, the goddess of wisdom, courage, love, and justice, breaks this impasse in the male psyche to get the story moving. With great compassion for the pain in Odysseus' divided family, Athena spurs each member to seek connection and reconciliation. In disguising herself as various men, she symbolizes feminine consciousness entering and influencing the male psyche. In time, Athena's feminine consciousness softens the overly masculine Odysseus, gradually awakening the tender, intuitive, and spiritual possibilities of his heart. As this implies, it is the arche-typal call of love in the aging male psyche that initiates the journey home. We have been task driven for too long.

Another archetypal theme in *The Odyssey* is a young man's search for his father. Telemachus wants to know his father better, secretly hoping for his love, guidance, and encouragement. While sons rarely really find the intimacy they seek with their actual fathers, their search for male mentoring is part of the growing-up process. In our story, Odysseus selected Mentor, an old wise and trusted friend, to look after his son and his estate while he was away. Athena disguises herself as Mentor to inspire Telemachus to search for his father and his own truth. We can conclude, therefore, that a mentor is a man who is open to his feminine consciousness in the service of helping a younger man find his way.

The goddess Calypso, who holds Odysseus captive, represents some kind of distracting "paradise" in a man's life – whatever has falsely captured the heart and prevented him from resuming the journey home. As such, she may symbolize a real or imagined affair, another exciting work project, or a new hobby, but she cannot in truth resolve his longing for home. We will return to Calypso's contribution to Odysseus' journey later in the story.

Discussion. What does it mean to come home? That is a question every man must ask and answer for himself. But one of the common themes is this: *You come home when you give up being the warrior and long for a deeper and more loving relationship with the world.* Male roles more appropriate to this time of life now call to you, like elder, sage, grandfather, gardener, and artist, all stirred by the restless energies of love. Though we may not like the feelings of helplessness that arrive with aging bodies, bodies that tell us that fighting now is risky, foolish, and immature, we will only know the wisdom of the next stage when warrior values are surrendered and the heart opens.

Nearly every man I interviewed spoke of his longing for family – for loving time with spouse, children, grandchildren, siblings, and friends. These men want to guide, encourage, inspire, and help their children and grandchildren. They want their partner to be happy and their relationship fulfilled. Most seem to sense that time is growing short and that love now matters more than ambition and achievement. I found this kind of love with my grandchildren. I could play on the floor with my five-year-old grandson and his wooden train tracks for hours or follow my two-year-old granddaughter around the yard discovering bugs and birds and never get tired. I can't get enough time with my older granddaughter or new grandson. I am not trying to be a "good" grandparent; I have been taken over by love. It has broken through the chains of achievement.

A question we sometimes ask at the beginning of this journey is this: *What is the value of personal growth in this final journey of age?* If you're just going to die, what's the point? When I posed this question to an older men's group, one answered, "If you don't continue growing, it's death, even if you keep breathing and walking." Life *is* growth, he clarified, and if this is so, then "not growing" is dying.

Men further tell me that the goals of this growth include knowing oneself better, exploring new values and interests, learning to love more deeply, caring for others, having a future to look forward to, and finding new rewards in life. As Odysseus will soon find out, aging represents a series of experiences and experiments, each with new lessons, insights, rewards, and growth. It's not over until it's over – keep growing.

The Challenge: Understanding the Meaning of Coming Home.
Whether you continue working or not, come home from the war before it is too late. Let love open your eyes to the joy and value of family, friends, and new life wherever you find them. You're either living or dying – which do you do?

Growth Questions

1 Have you begun to weary of the war? What are your symptoms of war fatigue?

2 Do you find yourself wishing that peace, love, creativity, and new interests could replace the demand for competition and productivity? What activities might begin to fill this desire?

3 Have you grown distant from your spouse or family over

the war years, withholding sensitive feelings, needs, and concerns? What is blocking your path home to intimacy and renewal?

4 Step back into this story as if it were your own dream. You are Odysseus far from home. Your wife and son are looking for you. You don't know how to get back. Where you are is ok, but something else moves inside you, a longing or tenderness that you haven't felt in years. What do you want most now?

Chapter 3

Early Mistakes

The Odyssey comprises eighteen powerful adventures, each symbolizing a developmental challenge confronting men on the long journey home. For dramatic purposes, Homer begins in the middle of these adventures with the earlier ones recounted during Odysseus' later visit with the Phaeacians. While this literary device may be skillful storytelling, it can leave the reader confused about the actual sequence of adventures. To remedy this confusion, I present Odysseus' eighteen challenges in their actual order of occurrence. It is interesting to note that Odysseus' eighteen adventures can be easily divided into four parts: *Early Mistakes, Transformational Experiences, Homecoming,* and *Final Challenges.*

We begin with Odysseus' Early Mistakes.

The Story. *The Trojan War has ended and Odysseus and his crew depart for home. The wind takes them first to the south coast of Greece, to a land populated by the Cicones. Odysseus raids a seaport, slaying most of the men, taking women as slaves, and acquiring considerable plunder. One man rapes a woman in the Temple of Athena. Rather than leaving quickly, Odysseus' crew hangs around drinking and slaughtering animals, giving the Ciconians time to send for help. A fierce fighting force soon arrives greatly out-numbering Odysseus' men. In the ensuing battle, Odysseus loses six men and the rest run frantically back to their ships, barely escaping alive.*

Interpretation. Odysseus resumes the same old pattern of pillage, plunder, and sexual objectification that marked his time at war. He has not learned anything new yet and simply continues his warrior ways. Though he seems to know when to leave, his men do not, symbolizing an early conflict within the male personality between moving on from the warrior life and getting drunk on more conquests and victories. The men who die symbolize the possibilities lost by foolishly delaying maturity. As everything in a dream represents part of the dreamer, so the Ciconian forces that drive Odysseus and his crew back to sea symbolize the fury of a man's psyche that feels betrayed by this return to savage warring. The plan was to go home, not start another war. The archetypal unconscious knows that the journey of aging must transcend such past behavior, and violently pushes the men on their way.

Discussion. Most aging men initially behave like Odysseus' crew. Never questioning their lifelong warrior ways, they continue pushing ahead in everything they do. In fact, nearly all men continue in their accustomed warrior mode at first because it is all they know. Trying to reinvent myself too quickly after retiring from psychology, I resumed all my compulsive habits of achievement and productivity with workshops, writing, and classes – changing the content didn't change the pattern. I was Odysseus ransacking another country. Similarly, many of my interviewees kept working in their chosen fields or, once retired, worked nearly as hard in volunteer, social, and recreational activities. Though claiming happiness, they have not put down their swords. I suspect we men secretly believe that either death or financial ruin will follow retiring the compulsive warrior, or maybe we simply fear missing future victories. Either way, like Odysseus and his men, we fail to grow.

Some of us also make the mistake of continuing other "wars" – with spouses, adult children, neighbors, coworkers, city hall, and imagined political foes. These battles can serve as defensive distractions from underlying feelings of failure, disappointment, fear, or depression. In this way, personal problems get projected onto others and we avoid the light of self-awareness. You don't change anyone else, especially with criticism and conflict; you can only work on yourself.

Age also influences how we approach this journey home. In their early sixties, men generally cannot relate to the aging tasks presented here or the over-arching goal of coming home from the war. They still feel pretty immortal. Until men experience the reality of aging bodies and accept the inevitability of personal death, Odysseus' adventures merely represent a good story. For the same reason, the earlier men retire, the longer it may take them to work through these challenges, for the "young" old have not yet felt the shudder of age. Age is a force that changes us, but it acts through the first-hand knowledge of physical decline and personal mortality.

It is not that continuing to work is wrong; only that it may prevent a man from facing the developmental tasks and opportunities of aging until much later in life, when he may not have the time, energy, or wisdom to benefit from new experiences and lessons. A man needs to ask himself whether his old work or work style are more important than finding untapped creativity, growing his unfinished self, or deepening relationships with spouse, adult children, and grandchildren. A man who works to the end may never know what he missed and, as the story suggests, opportunities die along the way if one tarries too long.

A useful compromise for some men is to cut back on work and carve out time for new experiences. Unfortunately, for many this compromise simply continues the warrior work mode. These men say they're retired, but they're not. As we will see, letting go of our work identity, life-long habit of compulsive productivity, and warrior competition may be more difficult than most men anticipate.

Where is the Ciconian's anger in the psyches of men who persist in competing for status and spoils? Sensing that they are wasting precious time on increasingly meaningless goals, the anger can leak through in frustration, irritability, and depression.

In the story, it may be symbolized in the killing of six crewmen, representing fury at oneself for the continuing foolishness of more war. This kind of rage turns into depression if ignored too long. As we will soon discover, such self-directed anger can intensify greatly before a man finds the path of growth and awakening.

The Challenge: Repeating the Past. The first mistake we make on the road to wisdom and maturity is to not change at all but simply continue the warrior life of competition, achievement, performance, and self-aggrandizement. The story touches on this Challenge only briefly, suggesting that the psyche sees this "solution" to the problem of aging as no solution at all.

Growth Questions

1 As you age, do you secretly compare yourself with other men and fear that you are losing your competitive edge, status, or career progress and should be doing more?

2 Do you push yourself just as hard now as before even when doing volunteer or fun activities? Why? What happens when you try to change?

3 What happens to your energy and creativity as you continue on the warrior path?

4 Step back into the story as if it were your own dream. Imagine being one of Odysseus' crewmen drunk on power and greed. How does it feel? How do you act? Or become a Ciconian angry because this invading warrior has shattered your peaceful life? How does this conflict between more warring and everyday calm express itself in your life? Create a dialogue between these two sides.

The Story. *Grieving for their lost companions, Odysseus and his men are caught in a violent and supernatural storm. Their ships finally reach land where they rest for two days. Resuming the journey,* *powerful wind and sea currents drive the ships for ten days, finally depositing them on an island of Lotus-Eaters. The inhabitants of this island share the honey-sweet fruit of the lotus with their visitors. All who eat this fruit, however, lose the will to work and completely forget about their voyage home. To escape, Odysseus binds his intoxicated men to the masts of the departing ships until they sober up far from the shore.*

Interpretation. Diametrically opposed to more violence and pillaging is simply falling asleep. We can leave the warrior life but then lose our self in the soul-numbing opium of TV, computer games, alcohol, drugs, meaningless part-time jobs, compulsive exercise, or deadening habits. In the process, we "forget" about our homecoming and abort the journey altogether, sliding into a kind of waking unconsciousness. This adventure, too, is short because it so abruptly ends the journey.

Discussion. I know a man who begins drinking every day at 6:00p.m. and is completely soused by the time he falls into bed. Deadening mind, body, and soul, he has no contact with his inner life and the individuation drive that might reshape his final years. He will probably die earlier than necessary and miss the growth of self and consciousness that transform later life into a journey of love and spiritual awakening. I know another man who constantly pursues exercise, keeping himself too tired and distracted to face his growing burnout. He will keep himself numb until his depression finally rots the timbers of his personality or a health catastrophe befalls him. In my case, I found "sleep" through busyness, novels, movies, visits, and yard work – whatever it took to escape feelings of emptiness and isolation experienced after my premature health-related retirement. In fact, I "slept" for months before realizing what I was really up against – the complete erasure of my public persona, professional life, and personal income.

The Challenge: Falling Asleep. The second mistake we make is to slip progressively into unconsciousness and forget personal growth altogether. The mistake of falling asleep is as dangerous as the mistake of continuing the warrior life. Both styles represent simplistic solutions to the challenge of aging, providing the illusion of a solution while secretly smothering genuine growth. Either way, a man does not know what he is missing.

Growth Questions

1 What activities put you to sleep these days?
2 Do you sometimes turn to numbing habits like TV, video games, alcohol, or exercise when anxiety, depression, or worry make feel you uncomfortable?
3 How might you force yourself to stay conscious in order to escape these addictive activities and identify the feelings that drive them?
4 Step back into the story as if it were your own dream. Imagine eating the sweet fruit of the lotus. How do you feel? Why is this feeling so powerful and so dangerous? Or feel yourself strapped to a ship's mast going through withdrawal. How do you feel as the drug wears off?

The Story. *Odysseus and his men now reach a place they describe as the "country of the lawless outrageous Cyclopes who, putting all their trust in the immortal gods, neither plow with their hands nor plant anything, but all grow for them without seed planting, without culti- vation"* (Lattimore, p. 140). *The topsoil is rich, rain plentiful, fruit is always in season, wild goats abound, and no humans disturb this natural peace. These Cyclops have no need for ships nor do they organize institutions and counsels, for each is a law unto himself.*

Shrouded in mist, the ships move blindly into the harbor as if guided by a god, arriving on shore hardly knowing how they got there. They feast on goats and sweet wine from their first raid. The second morning, Odysseus and a handful of men set out to explore the island. They come upon a cave and wherein dwelled a "monster of a man", a Cyclops named Polyphemus, who could be seen herding his flocks in the distance. Huge, powerful and ugly, he is a natural wonder to behold.

Taking twelve of his best men, Odysseus enters the cave. With the Cyclops away, they roam freely and find an abundance of cheese, lambs, milk, and animal pens. His men beg to leave for the safety of the ships but Odysseus refuses and builds a fire instead. They eat while awaiting the Cyclops, who returns to unload wood and perform various chores unaware of his guests. Upon spotting them, Polyphemus asks questions about their journey but Odysseus instead requests food and shelter in the name of Zeus. The Cyclops angrily retorts that he could care less about Zeus or the other gods and demands to know where their ships anchor. Odysseus lies, saying Poseidon had destroyed their vessels, whereupon the Cyclops jumps up, grabs two men, kills, butchers and eats them for his supper, blocks the entrance, and goes to sleep. Overpowered by this monster, the men wait until morning.

The next day, the Cyclops does his chores, eats two more men, and leaves the cave, closing the entrance with a huge stone. Odysseus then conceives a plan. He sharpens a large stick and hides it until later. The Cyclops returns, completes his chores, and kills two more men for dinner. Odysseus offers the Cyclops wine. Pleased with its taste, the monster drinks heavily. Odysseus tells the Cyclops that his name is "Nobody" after which the Cyclops passes out. Once asleep, Odysseus and his men recover the sharpened beam, light its point in the fire, and ram it in the Cyclops' single eye, blinding him and provoking terrible screams of pain. Other Cyclops living nearby, hear the cries and ask their friend what is wrong. The Cyclops replies, "Good friends, Nobody is killing me." Confused by this statement, the others assume their friend is alone and return to their business.

Despite his pain, the Cyclops blocks the door with the boulder forcing Odysseus to devise yet another trick. He and his men weave baskets to attach under the bellies of Cyclops' sheep. At dawn, the Cyclops allows his sheep to leave the cave. As the Cyclops feels only the

tops of the sheep, everyone escapes. The Cyclops even speaks affection-
ately to his favorite ram as he exits the cave, unaware that Odysseus
hangs beneath.

Back on their ships sailing away from the island, Odysseus shouts
at the Cyclops, taunting him with the fact of their escape. The Cyclops
breaks off the peak of a mountain and furiously throws it toward the
voice, nearly hitting the ship. When they get further out, Odysseus,
despite his crew's warning, calls out again to taunt the beast, bragging
of his trickery. Full of rage, the Cyclops calls out to his father, who
happens to be Poseidon, king of the oceans, to destroy Odysseus' ships
and throws one last boulder, barely missing his target.

Interpretation. How does this bizarre adventure relate to aging?
What might the Cyclops represent in the male psyche? Why has
Odysseus come into this cave and provoked such a monster?
Play with your associations and imagination for a while, enter
the cave, and move inside the drama.

In the story, we learn that Odysseus has been divinely guided
to a strange new place where he meets an "uncivilized" one-eyed
being. The divine guidance suggests that this meeting has been
ordained for his benefit – he needs to learn something here.
Despite the creature's size, Odysseus' descriptions of the Cyclops
remind me of a young child (do you remember the cartoon
character Baby Huey?) Specifically, the divine provides everything the creature needs and he seems most content with this
"magical" arrangement. His single eye symbolizes the kind of
wide-open awareness that exists in toddlers before the
conceptual mind locks in the duality of thought *and* perception –
it is an early kind of unity consciousness. Similarly, lacking
depth perception, he does not see past the surface of things and
is rather simple minded and naïve as a result. Like a child, the
Cyclops' emotions are primitive and uncontrolled, erupting
easily when frustrated or provoked. Eating men may symbolize
an early stage of psychological development where the world is

explored, and sometimes attacked, with the mouth. The Cyclops speaks warmly and affectionately of his favorite Ram, as a child might speak to his favorite toy, and lives peacefully in the sunshine of his simple life, engaged in parallel play with other Cyclops as young children play with each other. In summary, the Cyclops' island is a glimpse of the Eden-like paradise known in early childhood. Our hero has met his own immature, egocentric and emotional self – the two-year-old within.

We each have an "inner child" with simple needs for attention, dependency, and love. This young self embodies our most basic longings for security, affection, and love. Men, disciplined to be fearless and independent, however, will view this needy self as weak, unacceptable, or even disgusting. In the harsh light of their criticism, the young self appears monstrous, uncivilized, immature, and foolish.

Odysseus is curious and threatened, fascinated and repulsed, by this freaky and uncanny self-reflection. Like the bully who picks on vulnerable children because they mirror his own unconscious feelings of shame and inferiority, Odysseus taunts and embarrasses the simple Cyclops. In humiliating the creature, he is taunting himself, jabbing sharp judgmental invectives at his own simplicity. His disdain eventually provokes an infantile rage and a child-like call to "daddy" Poseidon for revenge. Blinding the Cyclops, Odysseus is really blinding himself because he is not ready to face his own infantile immaturity. Also, like the men hiding under the sheep, he hopes to "pull the wool" over the Cyclops blind eye. On the positive side, however, Odysseus is beginning to risk "going within" to understand himself (though he runs out pretty quickly!). He is beginning to work on himself.

Discussion. After a lifetime of living in one version or another of the warrior persona, most men have not spent much time with the emotional self within. When the warrior armor is removed, that self may feel and act pretty young. I have seen men break down and cry when their golf game fails. I have seen men explode in rage when narcissistic needs for praise and admiration are ignored in the invisibility of retirement. I have seen men collapse in depression when they feel rejected or dismissed by family members they ignored for years. I have seen men bristle angrily when asked how they really feel about aging, unwilling to face their fear and vulnerability. These men are wrestling with the Cyclops within.

As neither compulsive warring nor soporific habits solve the problem of aging, we must eventually look within and nourish our emotional growth. How do I really feel? What am I most afraid of? What childhood wounds now lie exposed when I can no longer hide behind my masks of superiority and productivity. An emotional youngness often lies behind the façade of power, importance, and competence found in the workplace. Remove the façade, scratch the surface with criticism, trigger humiliation, and an emotional "monster" sometimes bursts out.

The Cyclops in me has always been the young child dismissed by his overwhelmed, eruptive and disinterested mother. With five young sons and little time for her own ambitions, she wanted her life back. Fearing greater rejection, I hid behind a compliant posture, accepting the roles and expectations I was given, in betrayal of my natural self and its unfolding nature. Only later did I discover the aptitudes and strengths I had disavowed in order to keep peace. Now, when I enter the cave within, I find that the young child has become a young man. While the mirror reveals an aging countenance, the inner self is still vibrant and energetic. I now like and protect this ageless self.

The Challenge: Loathing the Young Self. The third mistake we make early in our aging is to approach our young, immature, emotional self with arrogance, disdain, and loathing. The challenge here is to avoid re-imposing warrior expectations on ourselves as we begin the inner journey of growth. While parents, teachers, peers, co-workers, or society inflicted such expectations on us in the past, we must not enforce them any longer. Criticism and judgment stall the journey; compassion and understanding encourage it.

Growth Questions

1 When have you felt young, rageful or worthless in these aging years? How did you express these feelings?

2 How have you hidden such emotional vulnerabilities behind the mask of importance or superiority during your work life?

3 Can you accept the young, frightened, or dependent aspects of your self without criticism?

4 Step back into the story as if it were your own dream. What do you see? How do you feel about this monstrous creature? If you were the Cyclops, how do you feel about these men in your cave? What's it like to be taunted and blinded by rage? What humiliations come to mind?

The Story. *Odysseus and his men arrive next at a floating island enclosed by a rampart of bronze. The island's king, Aiolos, has twelve children, evenly divided between sons and daughters. With no other people on the island, he requires his daughters to be consorts for his sons. Nonetheless his family is wealthy, well-fed, and live in great houses. The King and his wife entertain Odysseus and his crew for a month, asking many questions about their journey. Eventually Odysseus asks for directions home. As a parting gift, Aiolos gives him a tightly sealed leather bag holding all the errant winds that might blow his ship off course, leaving only the West Wind to carry them home.*

Aided by the West Wind, the men travel swiftly for ten days. Odysseus, anxious to reach home as quickly as possible, refuses to sleep and sails the ship all the way by himself. Just as Ithaca comes into sight, he falls asleep. His men grow curious about the bag and suspect it might hold treasures from King Aiolos or previous benefactors. While

Odysseus sleeps, the men open the bag, releasing powerful winds that sweep them all the way back to Aiolos' island. When Odysseus discovers what has happened, he is nearly suicidal with grief and remorse.

Odysseus returns to Aiolos' castle. He laments of his poor fortune and begs for the king's assistance once again. This time, instead of embracing Odysseus, the king orders him to leave the island, proclaiming that any man whom the gods punish with such bitterness will not receive his help.

Interpretation. In this fourth challenge, we meet a king and his family who appear to be totally self-contained on an island with impenetrable ramparts. Even the children marry each other, needing no other suitors, and everything is provided for them. This land is a powerful symbol of narcissistic self-sufficiency: the idea that one can – and should! - handle everything by oneself. That the island is untethered suggests that this defensive attitude is ungrounded; the inhabitants' strength comes not from a connection to the deep self but instead from rigid and superficial standards of self-sufficiency.

So it is that Odysseus, from this position of self-sufficiency, insists that he sail the ship single-handedly for ten days without sleep. Fueled by grandiosity and sheer will-power, he is once again the compulsive warrior doing it all. Odysseus falls asleep because he is, in fact, not emotionally ready to be home, given all the chaotic and immature emotions he has stuffed in the bag. The men who break into Odysseus' bag represent the greediness behind this grandiosity. So great is the emotional turmoil released from the bag that it blows them all the way back to the island of self-sufficiency, whose king now refuses any further help – self-sufficiency turning on itself. As symbolized by the king's reaction, Odysseus rejects himself again for failing.

Discussion. Many men push themselves as relentlessly in their aging as they did through their career. They believe that one more great work, discovery, or business venture will bring them the self-esteem and admiration they have been seeking all their lives. Others are just afraid to stop pushing, for they fear the shame of non-productivity, insufficiency, dependency or failure.

In the emptiness of my own sudden and premature retirement, I pushed myself tirelessly to reconstruct bronze ramparts of success and self-sufficiency, earning a second doctorate and attending an interfaith seminary. I had to find a shiny new identity and admirable way of life. It was not that these achievements were wrong – I did indeed find a new path in retirement, but the way I went about this quest was unmercifully demanding of my wounded self. Like Odysseus, I stuffed my feelings of failure and insignificance and sailed on uncompromisingly to a new shore – but it was not home, and when I opened the bag, I was blown all the way back to the original pain and confusion of retirement. Self-sufficiency had not solved the problem.

On a larger scale, the pain of self-rejection accumulating during a lifetime of heroic self-sufficiency cannot be "bagged" without terrible consequences – depression, illness, and empty relationships. We must open the bag of discarded feelings and needs and deal with them kindly. Like the truck driver who pushes himself with methamphetamines to complete long routes without sleep, when his bag of accumulated self-denial and abuse finally opens, out bursts a raging storm of suffering. We cannot come home to intimacy, love, creativity, and spirituality unless we dismantle the fortress of stoic self-sufficiency. And until we address our stuffed feelings and inner conflicts, they will create emotional storms that blow us far from the shores of love.

The Challenge: Demanding Extreme Self-Sufficiency. Another common mistake men often make is to try too hard. We believe that if we just push ourselves hard enough, we'll reach our goals by will-power alone. We refuse to let ourselves be *transformed* by the journey and thus approach home unchanged, a self-deception that simply does not work. Taking down the defensive walls and opening the bag of feelings, on the other hand, allows an authentic connection to self, soul, and the inner life that will awaken the energies of transformation.

Growth Questions

1 What are your ramparts of invulnerability? How does your heroic self-sufficiency manifest? What have you been pushing yourself to pursue without rest?
2 What "unacceptable" feelings of insufficiency, inadequacy, or inferiority are stuffed in your emotional bag?
3 What needs or feelings are you most afraid of sharing? Why?
4 Step back into the story as if it were your own dream. Feel yourself rowing tirelessly to get home. What's that like? Become the bag of winds. How do you feel bound up with such powerful energies inside? Become the sailors greedily untying the bag. Feel their shock when in opens. Then find yourself back at the fortress island realizing that the journey has failed or taken a detour. How does that feel? Or imagine you actually arrive home with this storm-filled bag. Does it affect your reunion with Penelope? How?

The Story. *For seven days, Odysseus and his crew sail on. Weary and profoundly disappointed by their last failure, they arrive at the island of the Laestrygonians, home of giant cannibals who work night and day. The ships enter a glorious harbor with towering cliffs. More cautious now, Odysseus anchors his ship outside the harbor and climbs a rocky point for observation. He then sends three men to enter the village.*

Odysseus' men meet the king's daughter, who leads them to her father's house. There they encounter a woman the size of a mountain peak who immediately calls her husband. He arrives, takes one of the men for dinner, and the other two flee in terror to warn Odysseus. The king raises an alarm and soon thousands of giants are descending on the men. Many are killed for a feast and eleven ships are lost; only Odysseus' black vessel survives, frantically sailing away.

Interpretation. The king and queen represent Odysseus' superego – the standards that form his conscience, and the cannibals symbolize his capacity for hard and tireless work. The king demands that the giant cannibals work day and night and he is furious when some nosey invader disturbs their endeavors. Exploring this island, Odysseus is taking another peek inside his personality to observe the structure of his compulsive work ethic. He is still learning about himself.

Upon arrival, Odysseus and his crew are deeply depressed. Once tantalizingly close to home, they are now as far away as ever. With the failure of his grandiose self-sufficiency, Odysseus - embodying the king's dictates - turns this work ethic against himself and his men are nearly consumed by gigantic self-hatred.

This time the primitive feminine, symbolized by the king's daughter and his explosive wife, triggers the attack. These hateful feminine figures represent Odysseus' inability to respond to his failure with compassion, love, and forgiveness – qualities of the mature feminine. Instead, Odysseus runs from insults the size of mountain peaks. Only as his feminine side matures in later adventures will we see the evolution of healthy self-love and maturity.

Odysseus barely escapes this encounter with self-hatred, and much of his power and self-importance, symbolized by his ships and men, have been destroyed in the process. Interestingly, this defeat provides the much-needed experience of humility, a requisite condition for genuine emotional growth.

Discussion. When their life-long self-sufficiency fails, men sometimes turn against themselves with gigantic and scathing self-hatred. It's not just one failure they perceive now; it's the failure of their whole lives. In shame and rage they attack themselves mercilessly, hurling personal insults the size of mountains because they have failed their own heroic standards of success, accomplishment, and superiority. Often this process is defensively muted and denied so that all you see on the surface are signs of depression – sorrowful expressions, low self-esteem, irritability, social withdrawal, or substance abuse, because admitting depression is tantamount to more failure. They carry their sadness alone, toughing it out "like a man".

There were many times I turned against myself in retirement. Despite the fact that factors beyond my control ended my career, I felt the crushing assault of self-hatred eating me for months. Blame ("I am at fault - I should have keep going at any cost"), regret ("I miss my old life so much") and self-denigration ("I am nothing now") destroyed many ships in my ego's armada, ships with names like strength, income, respect, control. Perceived failures of masculine self-sufficiency provoke such attacks from the workaholic giants inside who devour our self-esteem with hateful criticism – one more consequence of a life spent as a compulsive warrior.

The Challenge: Turning Against the Self. When lifelong heroic self-sufficiency fails, we often make the mistake of raging at ourselves, unleashing the cannibals of criticism, blame and self-loathing. The growth challenge here is to manage this anger at your self with patience, understanding, and especially love. You cannot let failure eat you up. The real enemy here is the unrealistic, unforgiving, and even punishing performance standard a man sets for himself - the true self cannot grow under the threat of such abuse.

Growth Questions

1 Think of a recent occasion when you criticized yourself harshly. How was that self-hatred related to unforgiving work standards and subsequent perceptions of failure, especially the failure of grandiose expectation you had for yourself?

2 How would it feel to allow your self to be discouraged, despondent, or lost without judgment?

3 Can you imagine holding your young self in loving kindness even when you fail? Try and see what happens.

4 Step back into the story as if it were your own dream. Be the tyrannical king demanding endless production form his giants. Can you find this figure in yourself? Be a giant – huge and powerful – working tirelessly on the job. When have you worked like that? Imagine challenging this horde of giants – your immense work ethic – and having it turn against you.

Chapter 4

Transformational Experiences

Having survived his first five misadventures, and the universal mistakes and lessons they symbolize, Odysseus now confronts a series of extraordinary transformational experiences. These next five challenges provide the chemistry of his metamorphosis from arrogant warrior to loving father, tender husband, and awakened seeker. They will also transform his voyage home into a spiritual journey.

The Story. *After fleeing the giant cannibals, and greatly relieved to still be alive, Odysseus and his crew arrive at the island home of the dreaded sorceress Circe. They wait silently on shore for two days and nights, still in terrible anguish about coming so close to their homeland only to be blown far out to sea again. Eventually Odysseus climbs to a high peak to survey the island. On the way back to his ship, a great stag appears on his path as if sent by a god. Odysseus kills the stag, braids a rope of grasses, and carries him to the ship on his back. The men admire the handsome beast and then prepare a communal feast.*

The following morning, Odysseus realizes that he is now completely lost and disoriented. He has no idea where he is or what to do and his men still feel the grief of their recent failure. Homer tells us "the inward heart in them was broken" and all "wept loud and shrill" (Lattimore p. 157). Eventually Odysseus splits his crew into two divisions and sends one to the house of Circe. Lions and wolves, enchanted by the goddess' evil drugs, surround the house, wagging their tails like friendly dogs. The men hear Circe singing inside and speak to her. She invites them in but one man, Eurylochos, suspects treachery and waits outside to watch. Circe gives the others a drink laced with drugs. Soon they not only forget their homeland, they turn into pigs. Horrified, Eurylochos rushes back to apprise Odysseus of what he has seen.

Odysseus knows he must confront Circe and asks Eurylochos to show him the way to her house. Eurylochos pleads to be left behind; he is terrified of her powers and certain that Odysseus will not return. Odysseus proceeds alone. Near Circe's great house, he meets the god Hermes disguised as a young man. Understanding the danger Odysseus faces, Hermes gives him medicine that will block the effects of Circe's evil potions. Hermes further advises him to draw his sword and rush toward Circe as if to kill her the moment she realizes her medicine has failed. Later, when she invites him into her bed, he is to comply but insist that she remove the curse on his men and swear upon the gods that she will not use evil against them again.

All this comes to pass just as Hermes predicts. Circe is astounded that her potion fails, is terrified by Odysseus' enacted rage, and drops to her knees clinging to his legs in fear. She then remembers earlier warnings from Argeiphontes, another name for Hermes, that the great Odysseus would one day visit on his way back from Troy, and asks him to share her "bed of love, that we may have faith and trust in each other" (Lattimore p. 161). After their lovemaking, four maidservants, water nymphs, bathe and anoint Odysseus and a feast is served, but he cannot rejoice. As directed by Hermes, Odysseus insists that Circe return his men to normal, which she does, and they now appear younger, taller, and more handsome than before. Circe asks Odysseus to invite his other men to her home. They are overjoyed to see him alive and even more excited to hear that their companions are neither pigs nor dead. Eurylochos, however, is so fearful and reluctant to return to Circe's house that Odysseus must restrain an impulse to cut off his head – instead he leaves him behind.

The crewmembers happily reunite in Circe's house and partake in a great feast. With Circe's urging, they remain in her house for a year, but eventually their homesickness returns. Odysseus entreats Circe to let them leave. In sympathy and understanding, she agrees but adds that they must visit Hades on their way home and there consult with the blind seer Teiresias. Odysseus weeps in despair, for no one has ever visited Hades and returned alive. Circe tells him to trust the winds, find *a thickly wooded shore, proceed to two thunderous rivers, dig a pit into Hades, and offer prayers and sacrifices to the dead. Circe also warns the men about the next three dangers – the Sirens, the strait of Skylla and Charybdis, and Hyperion, land of the Sun God. Understanding their fateful mission, the men leave, though one young man, half asleep, blunders off the edge of a roof and dies, his soul going directly to Hades.*

Interpretation. In this adventure, Odysseus comes face to face with the archetypal feminine – a goddess of great power and beauty. Crafty and dangerous, she seems more than a match for any man. If Odysseus is coming home to love, however, he needs to understand what the feminine presence is all about – an encounter every man must work out for himself. Because Odysseus is now profoundly lost and disoriented in his journey, he needs help from outside his normal masculine goal orientation – he needs to meet his feminine side as ally and friend.

Before confronting Circe, Odysseus slays a great stag presented by the gods (or perhaps is a god in disguise) and brings it to his men for ceremonial feasting. This act suggests the symbolic honoring, transformation, and internalization of the mature masculine archetype, symbolized by the stag, in preparation for meeting the feminine one. Once centered in his own archetypal masculine ground, he can approach the feminine.

As we will see, the feminine moves throughout this myth – beginning with the goddess Athena and ending with the mortal Penelope. In this story of the male psyche, females represent what psychoanalyst Carl Jung called the *anima*. Carrying quintessential feminine qualities of emotion, relationship, and connection, the anima represents both a man's inborn capacity to love and the soul mate he searches for to reflect the feminine side of himself. As the masculine archetype acts in the outer world of quests and conquests, she moves in his interior, serving as guide to his feelings, psychological complexes, and collective unconscious, like Dante's Beatrice. If the ego is the archetype of the ambitious, worldly, and action-oriented hero, the anima is the archetype of life, love, union, and the inner journey.

Despite decades of outer life experience, many men coming home from the war have not explored their inner world of feminine symbols and experiences very deeply if at all. When they pull back the curtain, they often discover rather primitive views of women that they have been hiding from themselves since childhood, views that also reflect the immaturity of their own feminine side. Like Circe, women can appear as dangerous, unpredictable, and powerful. In this part of our story, Odysseus must come to terms with the confusing power of the feminine.

There are many types of feminine power. *Sexual* power reflects the instinctual energies of sexual attraction and union. So much of life revolves around sexual longing, arousal, tension, and release. On the one hand, this kind of power can make men act like pigs and remain adolescents for years; on the other hand, a man's powerful alpha-male response to sexual arousal can become frankly dangerous, for dominant males compete fiercely for sexual supremacy in most mammal societies – recall that the beauty contest that started the Trojan War arose from this incendiary combustion of sex, aggression, and ego. Sexual power, in other words, can act like a drug in immature men rendering them foolish or violent.

Love, the second power of the feminine, is a *transforming* one. As Beauty transformed the Beast, so feminine love softens a man, gentles his soul, and awakens a tenderness largely missing in the heroic posture. This power is both inside and outside a man, part of his own inner feminine nature, and experienced via projection in the women he loves. The transforming feminine appears over and over in this story facilitating healing, growth, reconciliation, and love. She is Athena repeatedly whispering divine guidance to Telemachus and Odysseus; she will become Calypso giving Odysseus and his men the supplies they need to continue the journey; she is Penelope waiting with hope, patience and loyalty for her husband's return. As a man comes to know and express this feminine side, he grows in maturity and learns to understand women better. Experience with the transforming anima initiates him into this new kind of consciousness and capacity.

When men are afraid of feminine power, they unconsciously view women as all-powerful, like the cannibal crone in the fairy tale *Hansel and Gretel*, and with themselves as endangered children. Thus Circe initially appears as a witch-like sorceress, mixing potions and turning men into pigs. While this fear first arises in early childhood, its later expression in hate-based projections have justified all manner of irrational male persecution against women over the centuries – burning witches at the stake, blaming women for their rapes, and splitting the feminine into either saints or whores.

But when a man grows the capacity for steadfast strength, appropriate boundaries, even anger when necessary, along with an expectation of oath-like honor and genuine intimacy with a woman, then a new kind of relationship becomes possible, one based on respect, equality, complementarity, and love, one based on real women not imagined ones, and one based on choice. This is the growth that Odysseus experiences with Hermes' masculine assistance, the divine male teaching our hero appropriate masculine behavior and expectations with women.

Circe's counsel that Odysseus visit Hades represents a fourth kind of power – *intuitive* feminine wisdom. She understands that Odysseus must proceed further on his journey within, descending into long-buried wounds, the truth of death, and the resulting revaluation of life that a visit to Hades symbolizes. In other words, she leads him into an encounter with the unconscious that is both personal – his own repressed psychological issues, and collective – humankind's perennial and universal experiences with violence and death. She also helps him to anticipate three fateful challenges he will encounter after Hades.

Finally, *spiritual guidance* represents the anima's last power.

Odysseus' experience with the feminine becomes his initiation by the goddess. As the divine Athena and numerous lesser goddesses, she will help Odysseus resist the mind's illusions, encounter divinity, and journey to the psyche's holy ground. As the daughter of the most powerful god in the pantheon, she is the divine feminine guiding his fate. We will return to this spiritual dimension of our story when we discuss its ultimate lessons.

As a result of Odysseus' inner work, the feminine becomes his ally, an enormous achievement on the journey home. Now he can begin to embody her energy and consciousness, converting his customary fear and reactivity into patience and love. A new potential awakens in his psyche.

Discussion. I know a man who describes his marriage as a war that has never ended. His wife, a very wounded woman, reacts to him with explosive criticism, anger and blame. As a result, he is twice burdened, first by the immaturity of his own inner feminine and second by the immaturity of his outer one who behaves just like Circe did in the beginning. I know another man whose wife dominates their marriage and all their decisions. As angry as he feels, he always concedes all the while grumbling inwardly. Like an evil curse, these wars will continue until something breaks the spell, such as serious illness, separation, breakdown, or revelation. The hardest battles we fight, however, are often the very ones we need to fight – for in relationships, the real problem always comes back to *you*. If the fight were not pushing your buttons, the battle would end.

Men need to learn and feel genuine equality with women. At first, the forces of sexuality and love are so powerful they can derange a man. Until aging men revise the distorting images of women they unconsciously carry within, conflict and misunderstanding will continue in their outer relationships. But as men and women age, they each come into their own post-instinctual maturity, personhood, and sovereignty. Rather than playing out sexual, social, or historical fantasies, they become themselves, different in many ways, but friends and equals nonetheless. Then the witch, nymph, mother, and crone – the shape-shifting guises of the feminine in a man's psyche – gradually fall back into the collective unconscious from which they came. This, too, is the task of aging.

So it is that men learn tenderness with age. With the decline of instinctual male drives and the waning of the ego's importance, we tune into our feminine potential. We become more sensitive, compassionate, caretaking, inclusive, and loving. Most of the men I know will speak openly of loving and caring for each other as well as for partners and family. This is one of the great gifts of age, as competition for sex and power dissolve into universal love.

My evolution with the feminine seems almost textbook in its stages, projections, and issues. In early childhood, I felt cared for by the "great mother" as an all-knowing earth woman nurturing her young. Then, as conflict developed between my mother and I, she became the witch – terrifying in her anger and power. Unable to risk her temper, I lost myself often in her presence. Then, with the budding of "April love" in my psyche, I met the goddess as beautiful nymph and sweetheart – the pretty young classmate I fell in "puppy love" with in the sixth grade. The feminine evolved next into the alluring sex goddess of adolescence found in Playboy foldouts.

Adolescent encounters, however, taught me that love relationships were far more complicated and conflicted than my fantasies. A girlfriend could cycle through the archetypes of Earth mother, witch, nymph, and sex goddess, and the abandoned waif I met in break-ups taught me that my conflicts could be hurtful to others. The witch, however, caused most of the problems for me until I worked out my historical relationship with my mother. Then I found, as Odysseus did, my own masculine ground – my capacity to stand firm in the fire of conflict or leave when conflict became toxic. More recently I have met the crone – the wise old woman, and she has met the Senex – the wise old man. As we age together, my wife and I increasingly see each other simply as we are, without the overlay of projections. We meet in real life. And as testosterone levels decline, I tap into a capacity of love that seems almost bottomless – the inner feminine.

The Challenge: Coming to Terms with the Feminine. Odysseus must overcome the unconscious masculine habit of perceiving the feminine as a simplistic object or frightening threat and meet her now as a friend and ally, and then open to his own wondrous feminine consciousness. The world changes in this consciousness.

Growth Questions

1 Are your relationships with women changing as you age, no longer so heavily colored by flirtation, sexual fantasies, or fear?

2 How has competition and performance given way to love in your life? Where do you experience love most directly (grandchildren, helping others, music, art, gardening, other hobbies)?

3 What kind of wisdom is the inner feminine revealing to you these days?

4 Step back into the story as if it were your own dream. Tremble like Eurylochos in the presence of Circe the terrifying witch. How does she turn you into a pig? What does that feel like? Welcome the guidance of Hermes. Ask him questions about your relationships with women. What advice does he give you? Then stand up to Circe. Discover that you are not destroyed by conflict and watch how your relationship with her changes. Become friends.

The Story. *Following Circe's directions, Odysseus travels directly to*

Hades. They cross a wide sea, pass through a grim and wretched land of darkness and perpetual night, reach a stream called the Ocean, and find the entrance to a thickly wooded shore known as the groves of Persephone. At the junction of two rivers, one flowing from the river Styx, they dig a pit that opens into Hades. They pour offerings of milk, wine, honey, and water to the dead, promise future sacrifices, and pray to Hades, the god of the underworld, and to his wife, Persephone. With these offerings and prayers, they cut the throats of a ram and a black ewe and pour in a blood offering. Immediately the souls of the dead swarm upward in a frenzy.

Drawing his sword, Odysseus prevents the dead from drinking this blood offering until he can speak to the blind prophet Teiresias. Before he can do so, however, he meets Elpenor, the young man who had fallen off a roof and died as they were leaving Circe's abode. This lost soul asks for a proper burial, to which Odysseus consents. Odysseus then meets his own dead mother but is unable to speak with her. Instead Teiresias steps forward, drinks the blood (which apparently allows the dead to speak), and wants to discuss Poseidon's rage.

Teiresias reminds Odysseus that Poseidon's fury was caused by the blinding of his son, the Cyclops. He advises Odysseus to appease Poseidon and warns him to avoid specific dangers encountered on the Island of Thrinakia (described later). Teiresias then details a peculiar prophecy and related ritual: Upon completing his voyage home, Odysseus is to take an oar and go on another journey, traveling inland until he comes to a place where people know nothing of oars or the sea. There he will meet a man who will refer to his oar as a winnow-fan. When that happens, Odysseus is to plant his oar in the ground, sacrifice a ram, a bull and a boar to Poseidon, and, on his return home, render holy hecatombs (one hundred head of cattle) to the gods. The prophecy adds that Odysseus will live a long and prosperous life and die peacefully near the sea in "the ebbing time of a sleek old age" (Lattimore, p. 171). This prophecy will become Odysseus' final challenge.

Odysseus wishes next to converse with his mother. Teiresias explains that she, too, must drink the blood to speak. Odysseus asks her about his wife, son, and father. Hearing from her of their current circumstances and how desperately they miss him, Odysseus' sorrow intensifies greatly. His mother also confides, "It was my longing for you...that took the sweet spirit of life from me" (Lattimore, p. 173). Wounded by this crushing announcement, Odysseus tries to embrace his mother but fails because, as a ghost, she is completely insubstantial.

Odysseus now visits a seemingly endless series of deceased heroes and their wives, including Agamemnon, the commander of the Greek army in the Trojan War, who was murdered by his wife's lover; Achilles, no longer the fearless seeker of glory in war who now laments his own death; and several other famous heroes suffering their own unique punishments, like Oedipus' mother who committed suicide for the monstrous act of mistakenly sleeping with her son and Sisyphus punished with the task of forever pushing the boulder up a hill. As hordes of dead spirits clamor desperately around him, Odysseus flees in terror to his ship, commanding his crew to sail quickly down the Ocean River.

Interpretation. In this particularly long and moving chapter, Odysseus opens the gates of Hell for his next great transformational experience. It is a dark, powerful, and terrifying place. He has entered the realm of death and rebirth.

In Greek mythology, Hades is the god of the underworld, the oldest of three brothers who divided up the world: Zeus ruled the heavens, Poseidon the seas, and Hades the underworld. The dark and shadowed lands Odysseus passes through to reach Hades reflect the ancient Greeks' grim view of death. The mighty river Ocean, said to circle the world, bears a name universally associated with the unconscious, and as an offshoot from the river Styx that flows from Hades, implies that the unconscious and Hell are in some way synonymous. Persephone, as you will recall from another myth, was kidnapped and raped by Hades and taken to this underworld to be his bride. There she resides during the cold dark months of the year when the Earth appears barren and dead. For Homer, in other words, Hades, as dark god and gloomy underworld, represents a normally unconscious realm imprisoning the people, problems, and suffering from one's past, along with the reality of death itself.

Odysseus makes sacrifices and prayers in order to open the door to this underworld. Animals were sacrificed so their spirits could bring messages to the other world or as offerings to gain support or cooperation from the gods. Bloodletting was a particularly powerful ritual in the ancient world, for blood was a symbol of life. Letting the deceased drink blood was believed to briefly restore their lives, a potent incentive to come forward. Once the underworld was open, contact with its inhabitants could take place.

The ancient Greeks eventually ritualized the intentional descent into the underworld. Known as the pagan Mysteries, the ritual symbolically enacted the journey of death and rebirth as seen in the seasons – the descent of life dies in the autumn, the underworld of death through the winter, and the renewal of life in the spring. In essence, the ritual symbolized the death of an old life and the birth of a new one – the very definition of transformation.

Such mythic journeys to the underworld are found around the world. Psychologically, they symbolize the *death or surrender* of an individual's familiar sense of self, *descent* into the unconscious, *transformation* via contact with the powerful archetypal figures, places, processes, and themes of the underworld, and *return* to the ordinary world renewed or reborn. While Odysseus does not actually descend into Hades, as heroes do in other Greek myths, contact with its inhabitants is certainly enough to effect major changes in his attitude and values.

It is not surprising, therefore, that Odysseus would be sent to Hades for his next transformation. The myriad heroes he meets there represent virtually all the issues, dramas, and people from his past that he needs to come to terms with. Nor is it surprising that he should be referred to the blind seer, Teiresias, whose capacity for *in-sight* was as keen as any mortal's outer vision. Summing up all these threads, we can see that facing death initiates our hero's inner journey of transformation.

Like most of us, Odysseus cannot bear the power of this underworld experience for long and flees when it becomes too threatening. Nonetheless, we see that he has begun to question his own warrior values, observing that Agamemnon and Achilles, felled in their quest for power and glory, now suffer terribly for their acts, a sign of dawning maturity. He must also face how his warrior life affected his mother, wife, and son. He makes amends with the young man who died leaving Circe's palace and learns he must also appease Poseidon, whose son he blinded in arrogance – more evidence of maturity. As death changes all of us, this experience is changing Odysseus.

Discussion. Few men take the time to visit Hades. Sometimes prompted by a funeral or a depression, it is the painful but profound process of exploring one's own story, its wounds and mistakes, and listening for its deeper meanings, implications, and emotions. It also takes great courage to face the reality of personal death and the possible outcomes of your own foreshortened future. When you know death is coming for you, values and goals change markedly. Visiting Hades, therefore, represents a time of deep review, reflection, and reconsideration. It is a descent into our own unconscious and its contents. Taking stock so profoundly, a man grows real maturity and wisdom. The life born from this experience will be both precious and new. In one way or another, men need to "go deep" and return transformed – the ultimate meaning of initiation.

My own Hades came as a sudden and terrifying descent into the horror of anesthesia awareness. At fourteen, I had undergone open-heart surgery. During that surgery I woke up from the anesthesia to experience hands working inside my heart. Forty years to the month later, the whole repressed nightmare returned, triggered by atrial defibrillation in an emergency room. Like the goddess Inanna, I was called down into my own unconscious to bear this horrifying experience of personal death (Robinson, 2012a, 2012b). It was a death-and-rebirth initiation of the most profound magnitude I could ever have imagined.

The Challenge: Facing Death. In order to come home, a man needs to stop, take stock of his life, face his own real and inevitable death, search for his deepest values, and make amends for past mistakes. It is this process that makes a man an elder and grants him the maturity of age.

Growth Questions

1 Have you ever felt like some terrible experience or emotional state was taking you down into hell? What did you learn from this descent into emotional darkness and grief? What part of you died and what part was reborn?

2 How have previous identities, life structures, or friendships died in your lifespan and now dwell as if in the dark unconscious? Imagine visiting these former lives and learning from their experiences.

3 What past persona or event would you most like to revisit? What would you fear revisiting the most? Who from your past needs to visit you? Why would these experiences be valuable to you?

4 Step back into the story as if it were your own dream. How do you feel as you open the pit of hell? Who do you meet and talk with there? Take some time to engage these figures. What do they tell you? Imagine you ask Teiresias for a prophecy. What are you told? Where does the dream go from there? Imagine a soul journey into the underworld. Write it down as it spontaneously transpires.

The Story. *Odysseus and his crew return the way they came across the wide sea to Circe's island. As promised, he sends his men to the palace to fetch Elpenor's body and presides at a proper and heart-felt funeral for the young crewman whose soul dwells in Hades.*

The goddess Circe now addresses Odysseus and his men. She refers to them as "Unhappy men, who went alive to the house of Hades, so dying twice, when all the rest of mankind dies only once..." (Lattimore, p. 185). *Then, after feeding them, she tells Odysseus how to survive their next challenge - the Sirens. Enchanters of men, these mermaid-like beings sing so beautifully that sailors completely forget home and family, and are lured to their death. Circe instructs Odysseus to fill the ear canals of his crewmembers with soft beeswax to block their hearing. If he wishes to listen, she adds, he should tell the crew to lash him firmly to the ship and ignore all his pleas until they are well past the Sirens' call. The crew obeys his orders, allowing Odysseus to hear the Sirens' sweet song without surrendering to it.*

Interpretation. Continuing the theme of death, Odysseus keeps his promise to Elpenor and conducts the funeral he deserves. Circe comments that the crew's visit to Hades was itself a kind of death that few men choose to experience. This is a very interesting observation suggesting perhaps that in confronting our personal death, a second symbolic death takes place – we "die" to the illusion of immortality, a shocking realization! No wonder we fall for the Sirens.

The Sirens' song symbolizes the powerful and seductive fantasies we fall in love with in our later years to escape the reality of death – sports cars, younger women, world cruises, longevity schemes, cosmetic make-overs, the elixir of knowledge, and exciting new projects. We chase these fantasies hoping to preserve the illusion of youth and to delay death's visit. New adventures like these are not wrong but they can postpone our psychological and spiritual growth. Pursuing such fantasies, years go by and we forget the purpose of our journey - we were supposed to be coming home. Curiosity about the Sirens' power, however, leads Odysseus to risk hearing their song. He wants to understand the nature of illusion but wisely protects himself against its power – another sign of his growing maturity.

That the challenge of facing death is immediately followed by the challenge of resisting illusions is particularly interesting. In the first place, it suggests that illusions have been masking our fear of death all along. In the second place, however, experiencing the reality of death changes us. We cease to identify so completely with our customary sense of self for it will end; in its place we begin to sense a larger transpersonal consciousness – an omnipresent divine consciousness that permeates everything, us included. Mystics from every religion speak of this "death of the self" and understand it to be a pivotal event on the spiritual journey, but only if we see through the hypnotizing illusions that conceal our fears and imprison consciousness. Though few want to enter this passage - we'd rather chase illusions! - for the traveler who recognizes the importance of this symbolic death, an even more amazing discovery waits down the road.

Discussion. Fulfilling his promise to bury Elpenor may symbolize some as yet unfinished business. Even after visiting Hades, we may need to satisfy other obligations from the past. The psyche needs to wrap up the loose ends to move into the next phase of life. After making amends and paying debts, we need to stay focused for the next task on the journey.

If we run in terror from the reality of death, as Odysseus did at the end of the previous chapter, it is easy to be caught again by new illusions and miss the transformational power of aging and death. I know men who are forever setting new goals and campaigns, who race headlong into demanding commitments driven by the fear that retirement or slowing down equals death. I know men who pursue heroic quests - iron-man marathons and Everest climbs – to maintain the pretense of a never-ending future and the mastery of death. Doing these things "proves" you're not old. The paradox that each of us must face however is this: avoiding death in endless illusions lulls us to sleep; facing death awakens us to the infinite present beyond illusions.

I often fell under the spell of old fantasies disguised as new goals. Looking back, I see over and over that so much of my life has been an attempt to restore a harmony lost in childhood. Every new achievement, and especially every new quest, has unconsciously driven this fantasy – if I did enough, the love would be back. The achievements were still meaningful, but the hopes of the inner child of the past were never realized. In facing death, we see the futility of this childhood dream. What matters now is making love real in this moment, in this chapter. While new versions of old dreams can reactivate childhood fantasies, they will not end differently. Waking up from a lifetime of illusion is one of the great tasks of aging.

The Challenge: Resisting Illusions. Death draws near first as a friend asking us to take stock of lives, then as teacher reminding us of the impermanence of the self, and finally as a sage showing us something beyond ego. Death comes to awaken us. Don't hide in new illusions.

Growth Questions

1 How do you use illusions to flee the reality of death? What new fantasies, plans, and schemes maintain the illusion of your indefinite future?

2 You are going to die. How have you prepared for that? What do you expect will happen at death? Can you greet death as a friend and teacher?

3 How might *you* be an illusion? What would happen if you released this illusion?

4 Step back into the story as if it were your own dream. Be a siren and sing your sweet song of longing and love to the

tired warrior. What do you promise him? Become Odysseus strapped to the mast, desperately longing for the sirens' magic. What do you long for most? How do you feel when the seductive song has receded and you return to your senses?

The Story. *Circe now warns Odysseus about the narrow and extremely dangerous strait of Skylla and Charybdis through which he must pass next. On one side, concealed in a cave high on a cliff, is Skylla, an evil monster with twelve feet and six heads, each with three sets of teeth. Her heads shoot out of the cave like arrows taking six sailors from every ship that passes. On the other side of the strait dwells a ferocious Charybdis, a once beautiful water nymph that Zeus turned into a monster. She swallows and then regurgitates huge volumes of water three times a day, creating whirlpools that sink ships and spit back the remains. Near her huge mouth stands a fig tree.*

Circe directs Odysseus to guide his ship closer to Skylla than Charybdis while passing through the strait, for it is better to lose six men than an entire vessel and crew. At first Odysseus wants to fight Skylla but Circe warns, "Hardy man, your mind is full forever of fighting and battle work. Will you not give way even to the immortals? There is no fighting against her. It is best to run away from her" (Lattimore, 1999, p. 188). *Passing near Skylla, she does in fact lift six screaming crewmembers from their ship and eats them immediately.*

Interpretation. Circe, a representation of the feminine in Odysseus' psyche, has evolved from being a terrifying witch to a valuable ally. Mirroring Odysseus' own psychological growth, she offers him some very practical guidance. That he accepts her admonition against immediately fighting Skylla further illustrates that he is learning to manage his "hair-trigger" masculine reactivity.

Resisting the Siren songs of life, those illusions of eternal happiness we seek, is a profound challenge. An equally profound challenge comes in resisting our fearful illusions. Skylla's heads attack mercilessly from on high. She is the critical, threatening, and hateful intellect who kills with fault-finding, blame, shame, and fear. We can almost hear her words: "You're no good. You're worthless. You do everything wrong. You will fail!" Charybdis symbolizes the whirlpool of grief and depression experienced when we believe we have failed, leaving us feeling unloved and unworthy. Perhaps criticism, fear and depression also drive our need; our Siren fantasies. It is apparent that waking up from a world of illusion is critical to the transformational core of Odysseus' journey home.

Our work in this area is to prevent consciousness from being taken over by either set of illusions. Yes, we will sometimes hear the voices of self-hatred and defeat, but we don't have to believe them. Standing steadily at the helm while passing through the mind's negative illusions represents the passage of awakening. One of the great transformational experiences in life is to realize that self and world are not what we think. Odysseus maintains his concentration and skillfully negotiates this razor's edge, though he will return to it again, for we usually cycle back through this pattern several times to disempower it.

Any difficult choice can bring us back to Skylla and Charybdis because it generates new versions of old issues, that is, new illusions of imagined disaster. Passing through this "tension of opposites" happens when we maintain a clear and thought-free consciousness – what Buddhists call mindfulness – rather than being "consumed" by fear and depression. This birth passage of awakening is central to the journey of aging – there will always be more conflicts, fears, and defeats; coming home means transcending these illusions in awakened consciousness.

Discussion. Whether or not to retire, move, start a new career, undergo a medical procedure, or begin drawing our pension – these decisions can create the straits of Skylla and Charybdis associated with aging. Pros and cons are debated, fear and depression attend each imagined negative outcome, but the greater challenge is to recognize that these opposites are being generated from within. I know a man who wants deeply to retire but fears he will fail financially and be criticized by his wife on the one hand, or sink into a depression of inactivity on the other, for he does not know how to structure free time. He has never been able to support his own needs in times of conflict with his wife. He stands at the strait of Skylla and Charybdis. I don't know what he will do.

I sailed through the strait of Skylla and Charybdis frequently in the very experience of retirement – Skylla squalls that I am wasting time, doing nothing of value; Charybdis tells me it is too late, I am already a failure. We all create such tormenting dualities. One day, we stop believing that these illusions have the power to destroy us.

Challenge: Moving Through Fear and Depression The challenge here is to avoid believing the fearful thoughts and fantasies that lock us in the world of illusions. Yes, fear is real and so is depression, but they need not define or control our lives. The journey of aging is enlightenment in slow motion – and each time we move beyond the opposites created by fantasy and emotion, we are released into a world beyond thought. It is an amazing place.

Growth Questions

1 What fearful or depressing illusions are you most reluctant to give up? What would happen if you stopped believing them?

2 Can you see how thought, fantasy, and emotion take over consciousness? Try to experience consciousness separate from thought, fantasy, and emotion.

3 What is the hardest decision in your life right now? What

opposites characterize this decision? How might you pass through this strait without surrendering to either side?

4 Step back into the story as if it were your own dream. What free associations come to mind on these two monsters? Or become Skylla screaming at this foolish sailor? What do you want to do to him? Be the powerful churning pull of Charybdis sucking Odysseus' ship into its vortex. What noise do you make? What do you want to happen? Now be Odysseus. Hold fast the rudder. Guide your ship through these roiling waters. Can you reach the other side? How do you feel then? If you don't succeed, how, and why do you die?

The Story. *Both Circe and Teiresias warned Odysseus about visiting Thrinakia, the beautiful island home of the sun god Hyperion. Here goddesses care for seven herds of sheep and seven of oxen and, miraculously, these animals neither give birth nor die. But if any are slaughtered, punishment from the gods is harsh - the offender shall lose his ship and all his companions. Odysseus shares this dire prophecy with his crew.*

Odysseus and his men arrive at Thrinakia. A crewmember immediately complains that Odysseus pushes them too hard and asks for shore leave to rest and feast on Circe's provisions. Odysseus relents, extracting an oath that no sheep or oxen will be slaughtered. By evening, however, a gale of supernatural strength blows in, holding them on the island for a month. Eventually Circe's provisions run out. Odysseus prays to the gods for guidance but they bring him sleep instead. Meanwhile the hungry crew decides to slaughter some cattle for food. Odysseus awakens to the smell of cooking meat. One of the island's goddesses rushes to Hyperion and he in turn prays to Zeus to punish this egregious crime. Zeus agrees to destroy Odysseus' ship and his men once they are back at sea. The crew feasts for six days.

Leaving the seventh day, the men face a screaming wind that shatters their ship and drowns every last crewmember. Odysseus lashes himself to the vessel's keel and mast and clings for survival through the storm. He is eventually carried back to the Strait of Skylla and Charybdis where he grabs a branch of the fig tree and hangs onto it while the Charybdis swallows and then regurgitates his little raft. Climbing back onto it, Odysseus paddles for ten days until landing on the shore of Calypso's island.

Interpretation. In Greek mythology, Hyperion is variously known as the Lord of Light, the Titan of the East, or the incarnation of the sun. These references to light, east, and sun suggest the presence of divine consciousness and the related potential for enlightenment. An island where goddess-herded animals neither give birth nor die similarly hints of a supernatural realm free of birth and death, another reference to divinity. The number seven (seven herds of sheep and oxen, destruction on the seventh day) is often associated with religious beliefs (seven days of creation, seven sacraments, seven heavens, seven deadly sins, seven chakras, etc.). In summary, transcending the illusion of opposites, we have come to a divine realm, the opposite of Hades, a heavenly landscape with a profound spiritual lesson.

If the island of Thrinakia suggests the possibility of enlightenment, why does Odysseus fall asleep? The answer must be that he is not ready for the great increase in consciousness that arrives with the direct experience of divinity. While he sleeps, his men violate their oaths and incur the catastrophic punishment of Zeus. Odysseus' loss of consciousness, in other words, allows the lesser sides of himself, symbolized by his foolish crew, to act out his immaturity, invoking the awful prophecy.

We might ask, however, why the gods created the very desperation that led Odysseus' crew to break the commandment, for they were obedient until starvation drove them to risk the prophesy. We might similarly ask why the gods answered his prayer by putting him to sleep. Such paradoxes recall the similar religious question of why God told Adam not to eat from the

Tree of the Knowledge of Good and Evil in the Christian Genesis myth – it seems like a set-up and it was. Adam had to discover duality and leave the garden, symbolizing the humanity's inevitable evolution toward a dualistic consciousness: the cerebral split between conceptual and mystical forms of comprehension, between the left and right hemispheres of the brain. But our Odysseus has a different lesson to learn, one about ego.

On this divine island where there is no death, eating cattle is equivalent to putting the ego ahead of enlightenment, because enlightenment dissolves ideas of ego, mortality, and duality. The men's fear of death, however, aborts this awakening possibility, evoking instead their unexamined survival instincts. As a result, Odysseus is blown back to the strait of duality – the strait of opposites symbolized by Skylla and Charybdis. Put differently, you can't have ego (duality) and enlightenment (unity) at the same time. Unready to give up the former, he lost the latter and then nearly drowned in the whirlpool of depression. Nonetheless, Odysseus is shown the spiritual path – we must surrender everything we have if we are to experience enlightenment. And in aging, this surrender will eventually happen whether we seek it or not.

Discussion. Tastes of enlightenment are not uncommon in the spiritual journey, often breaking through at the most desperate times. Reaching bottom can push us through the final veils of illusion and we suddenly see the light. In such mystical experiences, we realize that the world and everything in it is in fact already perfect and divine, that we lack nothing and already have all we need. In other words, we are already on sacred ground. How might this happen to aging men?

Enlightenment can happen suddenly or gradually. The former is dramatic and unexpected, the latter more subtle and often overlooked. Let's consider that latter type in the following exercise: Let your mind relax and the movie reel of your life stop projecting its drama, and then simply experience what's around you. Not with your mind but with your senses. Examine whatever draws your attention – the way the light falls on the table, the sound of the air moving through the vent, the easy rhythm of your breathing, the angle of your sight, or posture of your body, the pen on your desk. Then ask yourself, "What if this is enlightenment?" Don't start thinking about this. Just focus. This sensory moment is the doorway to enlightenment. It always has been. This is it. In this thought-free consciousness, everything you examine is completely amazing, isn't it? It's actually divine.

I remember teaching a man how to experience mystical consciousness with four simple instructions: stop thinking, heighten awareness, experience the world exactly as it is, and come into the Presence through your own presence. He began to see how incredibly beautiful and peaceful the world already was. He began to feel happy for no particular reason. Whatever he did came easier when he wasn't thinking, planning, and preparing and imagining. He just woke up. And the world opened into Heaven on Earth. He had found Hyperion's island. Yes, thought returned and re-imposed duality, but he had glimpsed enlightenment and learned how to see in a profound new way.

In the progressive losses of aging, we surrender all we have, all we are, and all we believe. In losing these conceptual filters of the left cerebral hemisphere, however, we begin to sense, with the mystical perception of the right hemisphere, the divine world all around us and discover that it is always here, if we take the time to look. Identity, beliefs, attachments, and relationships, rather than being our ultimate security raft, create ego and its illusions – we cling to them and miss mystical consciousness. One way or the other, like Odysseus, we will be asked to give up everything we know and believe to experience the divine. If we proceed consciously, this capacity for wonder will ripen and allow us to let go more easily. The doorway to eternity is hidden only by the thinnest film of thought; one day it opens and you notice where and who you are.

There are two paths to enlightenment – resistance and clinging versus surrender and awareness. The first is the path of pain, the second of joy. Only by experiencing both paths do we ultimately learn the real nature of spiritual growth. The majority of us, like Odysseus, hold on to the rafts of identity and attachment, and miss enlightenment. This myth tells us that surrender will happen one way or the other for the ego is always defeated in the end. We continue in duality, however, because we have more to learn and because our spiritual work is here in the material realm of real people and embodied love.

The Challenge: Stumbling on Divinity. We cannot manipulate the divine for the ego's selfish purposes, but we can understand why the divine undoes our whole house-of-cards. To the extent that we can consciously surrender ego and attachment before death, we may find enlightenment expanding and reach the divine world right here as part of the journey. Consciousness can transform the world, opening the senses to love's imminence.

Growth Questions

1 How is aging gradually (or rapidly) dismantling your ego's security raft (health, wealth, beliefs, loved ones, independence, goals, and dreams)? In its absence, do you have glimpses or intuitions of sacred ground or higher purposes?

2 What is your experience of divinity? How do you believe the divine acts in your life, if at all? What do you imagine the divine wants from you in the journey home?

3 How do you move from resistance and clinging to surrender and awareness on this path of awakening? When has surrender given you gifts and insights you never expected?

4 Step back into the story as if it were your own dream. Become Zeus. Why do you destroy Odysseus' ship and his companions? What if Zeus symbolizes a higher consciousness that witnesses the little ego trying to preserve its narrow conventional world, which paradoxically obstructs its awakening? But keep in mind: this is a very difficult realization in the midst of terrible loss and will not make sense until a higher consciousness has evolved. Worse, at the ego level of consciousness, this realization can lead to self-blame, creating more Skylla and Charybdis illusions. As you wait for consciousness to expand, at least reflect on the implications of this realization. Consider writing a dialogue with Zeus about his paradox.

Chapter 5

Reaching Home

Following the transformational experiences of the last chapter, Odysseus continues his journey. All he has seen and learned, all the growth he has achieved in the previous ten adventures, have prepared Odysseus for homecoming, but he is tired. Stripped of warrior bravado and power, he travels on alone dependent on the gods and the goodwill of others to bring him home safely.

The Story. *After losing his ship, his crew, and nearly his life, Odysseus drifts alone and desperate on his small raft for ten days. He washes ashore on Calypso's island where he remains for seven years. This beautiful goddess falls in love with Odysseus and promises him immortality if he will stay and be her husband. Although the relationship works for a while, Odysseus grows increasingly homesick again. He misses his wife, his son, and his father. He desperately wants to come home but has neither vessel nor crew to resume his journey. It was this poignant dilemma that began Homer's chronicle and we return now to see how he resolves it.*

Motivated by deep concern and compassion, the goddess Athena pleads with her father to intercede for Odysseus. Zeus relents and sends the messenger god Hermes to Calypso's island to arrange for his release. Hermes finds Odysseus sitting on the beach weeping, his heart breaking in sorrow. Odysseus finally tells Calypso, "I myself know that... Penelope can never match the impression you make for beauty and stature. She is mortal after all, and you are immortal and ageless. But even so, what I want and all my days pine for is to go back to my house and see my day of homecoming" (Lattimore, 1999, pp. 93-4). Though bitter at first, Calypso grows sympathetic, releases her hold on Odysseus, and helps him build another raft to carry him home.

Interpretation. Odysseus struggles on and is saved once again by the feminine. The goddess Calypso rescues, heals, and renews Odysseus. She offers him immortality in paradise. She falls in love and wants him forever. She is the incarnation of the goddess archetype, the feminine face of God.

While he has not achieved enlightenment, Odysseus has found in Calypso the personification of divine love. She is the divine feminine in himself that he needs now to integrate into his personality and express in his life. But Calypso herself cannot replace the human feminine. As long as a man is mortal and still working out his life, he must find love with a real person and complete the journey home. As the story implies, the divine recognizes this imperative and frees Odysseus for the final leg of his voyage.

Calypso may be "perfect" but she is not Odysseus' wife. And her island may be paradise but it is not his paradise. That Odysseus falls out of love with Calypso and pines for his real-world wife, family, and home tells us that there is more to this journey of homecoming. While divine love transforms all it sees, you can't fall in love with yourself and you can't live forever. As long as you are a mortal and separate individual, the journey must continue toward a more natural ending.

Discussion. You can't retire in enlightenment and self-love can't make you whole. But sometimes we get stuck there. Sometimes we create "perfect" fantasies and try to hold onto them – as if we have found the goddess and she will love us forever. We find paradise in gated villas, expensive cars, second homes, fancy restaurants, ocean cruises, transient romances, second or third wives and families. But such "solutions" can only last so long before we pine for real relationships and real life. Sometimes this means accepting your spouse for who and what she is, and giving up the struggle to change or fix her. Sometimes this means surrendering the fantasy of a perfect life, another million dollars, or the final great achievement, and simply loving what your already have. I know a couple who can't stop earning huge amounts of money. They have so much but always feel driven for more. When "perfection" is an idea, it will never come to pass. The lesson of enlightenment is that you already have it.

In my own Hyperion and Calypso moments, the world became divinity and joy swelled in my heart. In fact, the spiritual exercises I developed for my Doctor of Ministry dissertation often led me to the literal experience of Heaven on Earth (Robinson, 2009) but I couldn't remain in this rarified consciousness – the world of problems and beliefs always descended upon me again. But more importantly, I didn't want to settle there. I wanted my family – my wife, kids, grandkids, and friends. I wanted to live immersed in human love. No longer focused on enlightenment or achievement, I now longed for relationships in this world. Heaven on Earth, I sensed, is revealed through this love.

The Challenge: Saying Goodbye to the Goddess. Fearing the end of life, we often make the mistake of clinging to a happiness that is only imagined. No matter how good it seems, the dream will turn sour. The journey goes on until we let go of illusions and come home to our own real life.

Growth Questions

1 Do you have a version of the "perfect" life? What would it be? How does it separate you from your real life? How do you hide in it?

2 What part of your heart's life do you pine for? Is there a relationship that feels unfinished or broken? What fear prevents you from coming home to it?

3 How might you ask the divine to release you? How can you release yourself?

4 Step back into the story as if it were your own dream. Be

Calypso brimming with love for this stranded warrior. How do you feel? What do you want from him? How does it change when Athena intervenes? Now become Odysseus. You have everything except your wife and child. Why do you long to trade paradise for a regular family?

The Story. *Odysseus sails for seventeen days on Calypso's raft when Poseidon spots him. Determined to avenge his son's blinding, Poseidon sends a vicious storm completely destroying the raft. With the aid of a sea nymph, who provides a magic veil of immortality for protection; Athena, who manipulates the winds and guides him through rocky outcroppings; and Zeus, who stills the water, Odysseus finally comes ashore on the island of Scheria, home of King Alkinoos and the Phaeacians. There he collapses in exhaustion, releases the sea nymph's veil, makes himself a bed of leaves, and falls into an exhausted sleep.*

Athena enters the bedroom of Nausikaa, King Alkinoos' daughter, who is soon to be married. Disguised as young girl, she convinces Nausikaa to wash her clothes the next day in preparation for the wedding. With a cadre of young handmaidens, Nausikaa brings her wash to the shore. After cleaning her clothes, the girls spend the day bathing, picnicking, playing games, and dancing. Hidden from the girls in dense foliage, Odysseus wakes up just as they prepare to go home. Like Adam, he is naked. Taking a leafy branch to cover his genitals and, looking quite frightful, Odysseus approaches the girls. All run in fear except Nausikaa, who an invisible Athena encourages to stay and converse with this man. Odysseus tells her of his recent suffering, begs for pity, and asks for directions to town and rags to dress in.

Recognizing his intelligence and superior nature, Nausikaa tells Odysseus about her land and people. She provides him with fine clothes and oils to anoint himself and, after bathing in the stream, Odysseus returns virtually transformed. Nausikaa, concerned about any scandalous gossip that might arise if she were seen with this handsome male, instead provides directions to her father's palace. She also instructs Odysseus to find her mother, Arete, and embrace her knees in proper supplication. Nausikaa then departs for home.

Alone, Odysseus travels to the city of the Phaeacians. Stopping in a sacred grove, he prays to Athena for assistance. She comes to him disguised as a young girl, praises the queen's background and exemplary social deportment, and gives him directions to the King Alkinoos' palace, spreading an invisible mist around him for protection from hostile inhabitants. Walking through the city, Odysseus observes its splendor and the refined qualities of the Phaeacian people. He admires their great ships and elegantly crafted buildings, fine clothing, and expert weaving skills. He learns that fruit from their trees never spoils and their fields remain lush through all the seasons. Finally reaching the palace, Odysseus begs an audience with the queen (who, ironically, is the granddaughter of Poseidon) and supplicates before her as instructed. Amazed at this strange man's arrival, and impressed by his gracious and cultured bearing, the entire court falls silent. Then the oldest and wisest man exhorts the gathering to treat Odysseus like royalty, and he is welcomed by King Alkinoos himself.

A grand and generous feast begins. The good King Alkinoos, greatly impressed with Odysseus, promises him conveyance for the final leg of his final voyage. The next day, the king provides Odysseus with a fine ship, fifty-two young crewmen, and generous provisions. More celebration and feasting take place. Listening to beautiful songs, Odysseus feels acutely homesick and cries silently beneath his robe. Competitive games follow, including foot races, wrestling, and boxing. Odysseus is encouraged to take part but declines at first, no longer reveling in such rivalries. Insulted by a contestant, however, Odysseus angrily participates one time, besting everyone with a superhuman discus throw.

Odysseus listens to a long and beautiful love song about Ares and Aphrodite and is entertained by wondrous dancing. He graciously praises the Phaeacians and the stately celebration continues with eloquent speeches, glorious presents, emotional testimonials and more music. Finally, the court asks Odysseus to talk about himself, his people and his land, and, in a long monologue, he recounts the long and challenging series of adventures encountered since leaving Troy.

Amidst even more gift giving, farewells, and celebration, prepara-tions are made for Odysseus' departure with the ship and crew provided by King Alkinoos. As soon as they set sail, Odysseus falls asleep, a deep and gentle sleep likened to death. When they arrive at Ithaca, the crew carries the sleeping Odysseus onto the sandy shore, concealing him and his gifts behind a tree, and return home. With Odysseus home safely, Poseidon complains to his younger brother Zeus that the Phaeacians should be punished for helping Odysseus escape his full revenge. After assuaging Poseidon's hurt pride, Zeus tells him to do whatever he wants to punish them. Poseidon transforms their returning ship into stone and roots it near the shore for all to see, fulfilling an ancient prophecy. The Phaeacians make offerings to appease Poseidon and avoid further punishments.

Interpretation. With Poseidon's horrific revenge, the destruction of his old life is complete. He has nothing. He is naked. He is humble. He begs for a young girl's mercy. Odysseus has dramat-ically transformed from the arrogantly judgmental and violent warrior to one who now pleads for pity and compassion. Aptly, the queen of this land is a descendent of the one responsible for Odysseus' destruction.

Almost like Adam in the Garden of Eden, the naked Odysseus finds himself in a magical place filled with abundance. Beautiful, prosperous, peaceful, and refined, this kingdom is as close to a human paradise as we have seen, reflecting Odysseus' own evolution and perhaps a vision as well of what might be possible if a mature and seasoned man returns home successfully. With the defeat of his immense grandiosity, a truly new stage of life begins.

The princess' forthcoming wedding and her delightful young handmaidens suggest the innocent bloom of first love and the uniting of masculine and feminine energies. Echoing the tale's beginning in *The Iliad*, this wedding celebration represents a return to the original theme of love and unity disrupted so long ago by warring egos. We are again reminded of the power of the feminine - Beauty transforming the uncouth Beast of Odysseus.

In this growing celebration, which anticipates Odysseus' homecoming joy, we find all forms of creativity – love songs, exquisite food, beautiful dances, eloquent speeches, grand architecture, intelligent leadership, and athletic prowess. Such creative expression reflects the spontaneous stirring and reawakening of Odysseus' inner life and his soul swells with images of family and home. Humbly kneeling before the queen symbolizes Odysseus' readiness to embrace family and love.

Odysseus now realizes that his longing for home will soon be realized. Despair turns to joy and celebration. He spends this interlude resting, enjoying, and preparing for his final voyage, though his homesickness never abates. It is also a time of remembrance, a time to integrate all he has learned and to understand it more deeply. As the happiness of the Phaeacians mirrors the anticipatory joy of homecoming, so Odysseus' many departing gifts, new ship and able crew reflect a renewed strength to cross the final threshold. Humility, kindness, creativity, and hope have revived his spirit. Trusting that his homecoming is real this time, and exhausted from his long journey, Odysseus falls into a deep sleep, like an infant in the arms of love, and awakens where his journey began so long ago – at home. It's as if the dream of transformation, like Dorothy's trip to Kansas, has now been completed.

Poseidon now wants to punish the Phaeacians for helping Odysseus escape. Why must they bear Odysseus' punishment? A clue can be found in Poseidon's choice of punishment: To be turned to stone symbolizes being frozen in terror – literally petrified – by the fear of sudden violent punishment. A child raised with violence will experience this terror often, and sometimes compensate for it by identifying with the aggressor, that is, becoming the dangerous figure he still unconsciously fears, continuing the cycle of violence another generation. This is probably Odysseus' story and one common to men of his time. Homer may be showing us that Odysseus, and most men, need to face this early wound. Making it into a public monument, as cultures often do to remember past violence, ensures that all men will be reminded of their shared history. Indeed Poseidon may symbolize the trauma of the violent male that warriors need to address to come home.

Discussion. We come home when we surrender attachment to our self-important identity and the warrior life. We come home when we are humble, grateful, and trusting. We come home when we finally understand where our journey has taken us and why. We come home when we realize that life is good enough just as it is. We come home when we resolve our earliest terror. From here, men feel like there is nothing more to prove, nothing to achieve or acquire, and nothing to stand between the heart and its joyful destiny. We turn now to creativity, gratitude, happiness, and love.

It is so interesting that Odysseus reaches this place of joyous celebration right after he loses the last shred of his egocentric control and grandiosity. But as we will see, there is yet more work to be done. In place of this happy fantasy of homecoming, a man's actual reunion with his former life requires significant housecleaning. Fantasy and reality are rarely the same. Still, the excitement and hope are real and provide energy for the final leg of the journey.

I feel the celebratory burst of joy every time we visit our children and grandchildren. I feel this joy when we "play" together with our friends – board games, BBQ's, dinners. I feel this joy on the "date night" my wife and I have reserved every Friday for thirty-five years. And I feel happy whenever I write a new song and play it for others. In fact, my songwriting output keeps growing and has come to represent the expression of my new heart-based creativity. All this is part of loving in the "Third Age".

The Challenge: Celebrating Home. If we understand that loss and surrender can be a path of personal transformation, then acceptance will reveal a new world right where we are. In giving up everything – control, riches, arrogance, even health, we see life as it is – already beautiful and full. Creativity flows from the soul, hope quickens the heart, and healing brings renewed joy, wonder, and purpose.

Growth Questions

1 Can you imagine the joy arising in this stage of the journey? You now know for certain that you will reach your heart's desire. What does this joy evoke in you?

2 Where has your creativity gone? How and where might it be revived to express your gifts and your heart's vision of life?

3 What do you want most when you reach home?

4 Step back into the story as if it were your own dream. Wake up naked on the shore lost and destitute. Feel the excitement of returning to civilization with new interest. Embrace these beautiful and graceful people and join the dance. Feel this celebration in your body. Imagine what your homecoming might be like. Sleep in happy anticipation of the new dawn.

The Story. *Odysseus wakes up but does not recognize his homeland, for Athena has surrounded him with amnestic mist. She wants to talk with him first before he returns to his palace. Naturally Odysseus thinks the Phaeacians have tricked him. Disguising herself as a young man, Athena approaches Odysseus, engages him in conversation, and finally tells him he has reached Ithaca. Though thrilled, Odysseus promptly spins a long and complex lie about his identity and recent* *adventures. Athena accuses him of lying, returns to her goddess form, and explains that she is here to help him and has, in fact, been aiding him and his son all along. Athena removes the mist and Odysseus recognizes his homeland and gratefully kisses the ground.*

Athena and Odysseus hide the wealth acquired from the Phaeacians in a nearby cave and begin plotting his revenge on the suitors. As a first step in the plan, Athena disguises Odysseus as an old beggar dressed in vile and squalid rags. They part ways, with Athena traveling to Sparta to fetch Telemachus and Odysseus going to visit Eumaios, the palace swineherd, an old and loyal employee, where he will hide until executing his plan.

Odysseus finds Eumaios in a humble shelter looking after the palace's stocks of pigs. Though Odysseus appears as a stranger, the swineherd welcomes him warmly and offers simple food and drink. Eumaios expresses tender concern for his absent master and his beloved family, and worries aloud about the trap the suitors have planned for Telemachus. Eumaios believes Odysseus has perished and the disguised Odysseus tries to convince him otherwise. Asked who he is and where he comes from, Odysseus weaves another long and complicated lie about his adventures in the Trojan War that the swineherd eventually disbelieves. Later, Eumaios prepares a sumptuous meal by sacrificing a prize pig. Intoxicated with wine and admittedly boasting, Odysseus spins yet another tale about saving a young man's life. That night Odysseus reflects happily on with how well Eumaios has cared for his estate.

Meanwhile, Athena travels to Sparta to urge Telemachus home. After telling him how to avoid a trap the suitors have set, she instructs Telemachus to go first to the swineherd and then home to reassure his mother that he is alive and safe. His reunion with the swineherd is warm and loving. In fact, Telemachus frequently refers to the swineherd as "father". Telemachus sends the swineherd off to tell his mother of his safe return, leaving him alone with the old beggar. Athena secretly appears to Odysseus now, telling him to reveal himself to his son, and removes the beggar disguise. Father and son embrace tearfully, crying deeply for all the time they have lost and the joy of their reunion at last.

Odysseus informs Telemachus of his plan for defeating the suitors, a plan his son initially doubts given their enemy's far greater numbers. According to the plan, Odysseus will return to the palace disguised again as an old beggar. Telemachus will tell no one of his father's true identity, silently bear the humiliation Odysseus will endure at the hands of the suitors, but secretly hide the suitors' weapons in preparation for battle. Meanwhile, at Odysseus' castle, the suitors complain bitterly of being outwitted in their plan to kill Telemachus and devise new schemes. Penelope, hearing this talk, rages at them to no avail, for they lie shamelessly about their love for Telemachus.

Telemachus leaves for the palace to comfort his mother. He tells the swineherd to take the "beggar" – Odysseus again in disguise – to the city. The mother-son reunion is also warm and heartfelt, for Penelope feared she would never see her son again. Protected by an "enchantment of grace" from Athena, Telemachus wanders the palace. Overhearing the suitors secretly devising more evil plans, Telemachus returns to Penelope and promises that his father will avenge her. Unexpectedly, a seer reveals that Odysseus is already in Ithaca, but Penelope is too afraid to believe this good news.

The swineherd now brings Odysseus to the city where they come upon the palace goatherd, an evil and disloyal man who insults, humiliates, and kicks the old beggar. Odysseus holds back his anger. On approaching the castle, Odysseus encounters his old dog, Argos, who has been neglected and abandoned, and lies riddled with fleas in a pile of dung. Despite Odysseus' disguise, Argos immediately recognizes his master and excitedly greets him, only to die soon thereafter.

Foul-smelling and disgusting, for he is still disguised as the beggar, Odysseus enters the palace with the swineherd and begins to beg among the suitors. Antinoos, one of their leaders, heaps more insults upon Odysseus, shaming him relentlessly and throwing a stool that strikes his right shoulder. Both Odysseus and Telemachus suppress their fury. Hearing of this indignity, Penelope asks the swineherd to bring the

*beggar to her that she might console him. The beggar tells her that he is
a friend of Odysseus, stirring her curiosity. Penelope invites the beggar
to meet with her again but he postpones their conversation until
evening, explaining that he wants to avoid any more abuse from the
suitors.*

*Odysseus soon meets another beggar who considers the palace his
own territory. He abuses Odysseus with violence and insults. Seeking
sport and entertainment, Antinoos sets up a fight between these two
vagabonds. The winner will be fed, the loser sent away. After first
seeking unsuccessfully to befriend this adversary, Odysseus agrees to
fight and reveals the powerful body beneath his beggar clothes, terrifying his opponent. Odysseus, however, withholds the full force of his
strength to avoid killing the man who is defeated with a single blow.*

*Meanwhile, Athena puts Penelope to sleep and makes her even more
beautiful. When she reappears before the suitors, their passions are
enflamed, setting the stage for a final competition for her affections.
Rapt with desire, the suitors send their servants off to collect fine gifts,
returning with precious treasures, and their cruel festivities resume.
Odysseus instructs the palace maids to serve the queen while he builds
a fire; they respond by laughing at him. One of Penelope's favorite
maidservants, Melantho, whom she once treated like a daughter, has
become a mistress to Eurymachos, a most powerful suitor. Melantho
scolds Odysseus, who responds with scathing threats, scattering the
maidservants. Eurymachos hurls more humiliations at Odysseus and,
feeling insulted by his retort, throws another stool at him. Telemachus,
growing ever bolder, sends them all home for the night.*

*After the suitors depart, Odysseus and his son begin their revenge
plan by locking up the suitors' weapons, after which Telemachus goes
home for the night. Penelope comes down from her chambers as
beautiful as Aphrodite for her visit with the beggar. Odysseus praises
her faultless loyalty and begs her not to ask him personal questions.
Penelope tells him of her fervent hope for her husband's return,
admitting her great longing. She then tells the beggar of the ruse she
uses to put off the suitors, promising to marry one of them of them upon*

finishing a shroud she is weaving for Odysseus' father. Each night, of course, she secretly undoes her progress. Sadly, her servants discover her ploy, forcing her to finish it, and now she must choose a new husband among the suitors. Odysseus weaves his own clever deceit, telling Penelope that he knows her husband and describes many of the journeys that he himself experienced. Penelope weeps in longing, not realizing that she is in fact talking directly to her long-lost mate. Odysseus hides his own tears.

Penelope then asks the beggar questions about her husband's wardrobe to determine whether he truly knew Odysseus. His correct answers evoke even more sorrow. Odysseus tells Penelope that her husband is safe and will be home soon. Inconsolable, she again doubts his veracity but asks one of her servants to bathe the beggar as an offering of gratitude. This servant, it turns out, is Odysseus' childhood nurse who excitedly recognizes a scar on his leg from a childhood boar attack. Odysseus commands her to silence.

After his bath, Odysseus resumes his conversation with Penelope. She describes a recent dream in which twenty geese are killed by an eagle. In the dream, she was told not to fear because the geese represented the suitors and the eagle was her husband home to avenge her. She also reveals her own plan to set up a contest among the suitors for her hand in marriage. The contest involves shooting an arrow from her husband's bow through the handle rings of twelve axes lined up in a row. Odysseus endorses her plan without revealing his motives and Penelope goes off to bed, weeping in sorrow until Athena casts the spell of sleep upon her.

Interpretation. In the twentieth year of his absence, Odysseus finally reaches home. In that time, his mother has died, his young son has grown to manhood, and his wife has aged in grief. By virtue of his many trials, however, Odysseus has achieved a significant measure of humility and self-control. Unlike his old self, trigger-happy and egotistical, Odysseus has learned to hold his punches, replace reactivity with reflection, and plan intelligently. Disguised as a beggar, symbolizing this new and far more humble consciousness, Odysseus travels first to his loyal swineherd and graciously accepts his meager hospitality.

The long reconnaissance and preparation described in this chapter have many purposes. Odysseus knows that he cannot simply show up at home and expect to be warmly welcomed. First he must deal with the dangerous and powerful suitors. As you will recall, these suitors represent the greed, ambition, and vanity of the warrior mentality – Odysseus' mentality! – that must be fully dispatched before rejoining home and family pure of heart. Like weeds, this complex of warrior thoughts, emotions, and behavior patterns have infested and dominated his psyche for decades. If Odysseus simply resumed his old role in the family, he would fall back into the same old habits in minutes.

Turning to the outer reality of the story, Odysseus, like all of us coming home, must build new relationships with his family. His son Telemachus has struggled painfully in his absence, and father and son need time to get reacquainted and to share their stories. That Telemachus is coming of age himself reflects of the developmental reality that the next generation is moving toward leadership positions in society so elders can move on to their next roles. Odysseus also reunites with the family dog and then sadly watches him die, a reminder that time is precious and aging and death await us all.

Penelope, too, has suffered greatly and Odysseus must face the hurt, doubt, and anger he left behind while pursuing his warrior life. The fact that she does not recognize him at first suggests that she cannot yet see who he has become in the trans- formational journey; she cannot appreciate his new state of consciousness. The idea of a contest between suitors for her hand suggests that the feminine wants to see which version of Odysseus will now show up. Will he be simply another arrogant version of his old self or a wise and loving man who can contain and focus his powers in the service of the heart not the ego?

. To understand the struggles of Telemachus and Penelope even more deeply, put yourself in their shoes. If you were Telemachus, how would you feel? Your father has been off fighting this war for twenty years. You have no memory of him and wonder if he is even still alive. Your real fathering came from the kindly old swineherd. Then this stranger shows up and says he is your father. A lifetime of feelings, issues, and questions need to be worked through before all is well. Moreover, if we understand this "war" to symbolize your father's emotional absence from home, how do you feel when he suddenly wants to be your friend? These same feelings, questions and issues arise in a marital context when you imagine being Penelope. Yes, your husband has been around, but psychologically he may have grown quite distant, and genuine emotional intimacy may not have existed for a long time. Are you ready to let him back into your life?

And still more levels exists here. If Penelope symbolizes a man's capacity to love held captive for decades by the suitors of career and ambition, how can he keep from returning to his former warrior ways once he returns? And if Telemachus represents his own young self looking for a father's love – the inner child ignored for two decades - what will prevent a man from abandoning that young self again in search of more ego gratifications? As you can see, the developmental task here involves a total reorganization of motivation and personality. Coming home is no slam-dunk.

Finally, if Odysseus is so much more mature now, why does he lie so quickly and facilely to everyone he meets in this initial phase of homecoming? Resourceful and cunning by nature, he watches people, sizing up their character, motives, and state of mind before revealing his own. But his reserve hides something else. Odysseus is afraid. He is beginning to understand the pain he has caused his family and does not know how they will react to him, and whether they still value, want, or love him. Instead of demanding respect as some men do, he wants to know if the love he seeks is still there. Disguised as a beggar, a symbol of profound humility, he is also trying to be as conscious, careful, humble, and respectful as possible.

Discussion. Many men return from the war thinking they can simply walk into their household and take over – husband as CEO. They retire without considering the family's feelings or how to cleanse their consciousness of a lifetime of warrior habits and fantasies. This lack of insight, preparation, and humility does not play well with their partners, who often feel angry, disrespected, or disappointed, and eventually encourage their errant husbands to seek activities away from home everyday, mimicking their former work lives. Nor do many wives recognize this new creature as their husband. He has changed from the one she married but who is he now? A time of waiting, observation, acclimation, and patience precede any authentic marital encounters for both sides, a time when wives "test" their men to see if they have really changed and men test their wives to see if there is any love left. Grown children, of course, have many of the same questions.

Some retired men, on the other hand, feel bossed around and supervised by their wives, as if she now functions as the CEO giving them "honey-do" lists and chores. Her controlling defense annexes her husband's power, as if she were saying, "I'm the boss now. Don't try to take over." Here, too, a man's adult children will have similar conflicts with his sudden interest in relating. "Where was he during my school years?" "Why does he think I want to be close now that I have my own life?" Take your time, men. Put your ego aside. Listen and watch until you know "what's what".

Coming home from the war also entails coming home to oneself. A man asks, "Will I be the old or new me?" "Will I be happy in this new life or feel restless and bored?" Each of us must take time to understand and remove our deeply ingrained warrior patterns or they will dominate us again. As you can see, there is a lot of work here. It is the work of coming home.

As I came home to my wife and grown children, I needed to put aside my strong warrior persona – the great provider mask – and expose the doubts, uncertainties, and confusion that lay beneath it. Who was I now? What was my role in the family? And who had my wife become? Like Penelope, she had also changed over the years, becoming stronger and more self-confident. This loss of traditional marital roles left me reeling and raised many unspoken questions. Who was I to her now? What kind of relationship would we have in this new era? Similarly, with my grown children, I wondered what was my purpose if I were no longer needed as provider, cheerleader, and coach? These had also been self-serving protective roles, roles that securely defined my place in the family. Now, like Odysseus on the shore of Ithaca, I felt naked and uncertain, and knew that every habitual reaction on my part was going to be wrong. So I waited, watched, reflected and, like Odysseus, began tentative and cautious conversations with my family to see what they wanted, expected, and felt in this new time.

The Challenge: Preparing for Homecoming. Prepare yourself with insight, humility, and self-control as you psychologically move home again. Be patient and give your family time to see who you have become and to reveal who they are now before initiating a new relationship. Your spouse or children may even pose "tests", consciously or unconsciously, to see whether you are different, whether you have matured, or whether anything has really changed. Are you really home or just pretending?

Growth Questions

1   How many ambitious "suitors" still hold your love captive in your psyche? In other words, how often do you find

yourself imagining more quests and challenges instead of living in the here and now with those you love?

2 Can you take the time to assess your place in the home, old and new, before stepping back in? With whom do you need to make amends or find forgiveness? How can you approach them without demands, presumptions, or expectations?

3 Can you let yourself be hurt or criticized without responding defensively as the family gets used to your really being home?

4 Step back into the story as if it were your own dream. Be Odysseus carefully approaching his home, cautious and disguised, testing the waters. How does your heart swell when you meet your son and finally reveal yourself to him? Become Telemachus. How do you feel in your father's arms? What do you want from him? How do you feel in Penelope's presence when you cannot yet reveal all you feel? And how do you deal with the ridiculing warrior voices inside your head judging you now as a nothing, a failure? Do you agree with them?

The Story. *Filled with nearly explosive rage, Odysseus cannot sleep. Tossing and turning in bed, he barely resists rushing out and killing every suitor in sight, including the treasonous maidservants who consort with the suitors and laugh loudly through the night. But Odysseus talks to himself, wisely counseling patience. Athena, too, comes to Odysseus, reminding him to be grateful that he is home with his wife and son. She also reassures him that, despite his fear of being outnumbered by treacherous suitors, he will prevail. At the same time, Penelope awakens in sorrow, crying loudly enough to awaken Odysseus, and both pray separately to the gods for relief and hope. Zeus, from high on Olympus, sends thunder down on Ithaca as an omen. A tired mill woman far from the palace silently joins the royal couple in prayer. She, too, wishes that the suitors, whose demands for* *ground flour have exhausted her, would finally leave.*

The next day, the suitors return to their drunken feasting and humiliate Odysseus further when someone throws an ox hoof at him. With his father near, Telemachus grows ever bolder, confronting the suitors, demanding their respect, shocking them to near silence. Athena secretly quickens the suitors' frenzied bloodlust. They demand that Telemachus permit his mother to remarry, threaten to throw him out of the palace, and continue insulting Odysseus. The tension builds rapidly.

Athena guides Penelope to initiate the fateful contest. Retreating to the innermost chamber of the palace where valuables are stored, Penelope finds Odysseus' great bow. The chamber door opens with the sound of a bull's bellow and Penelope weeps at what she must do. Arriving back at the banquet hall, she addresses the suitors, explaining the contest rules. Specifically, the man who can string the mighty bow and send an arrow through the rings of twelve lined-up axes will have her hand in marriage. Telemachus announces that he, too, will enter the contest, planning to keep his mother in her home if he wins. Telemachus sets the axes in the ground in a perfectly straight line. Three times he attempts and fails to string the bow; the fourth time he would have succeeded but Odysseus stops him. Telemachus admits that perhaps he is still too young to succeed and invites the suitors to come forth.

The first man tries and fails to string the powerful bow. A disdainful suitor scolds him and instructs other young men to heat the bow and rub it with fat to render it more pliable. Still no one is strong enough to do it. Odysseus steps away from the contest to meet with the swineherd and oxherd, both of whom he trusts, and reveals his identity. After a tearful reunion, he instructs them to return to the banquet hall, bolt the doors, and send the women outside.

Eurymachos, one of the most powerful suitors, tries and fails to string the bow. Antinoos argues that they should take a break and return to feasting. All agree and resume eating and drinking. Odysseus, pretending at first to agree, then asks if he might to try to string the bow himself. The suitors are furious at this outrageously disrespectful proposal. *Penelope intercedes, but the suitors again resist, secretly fearful of being shamed by a lowly vagrant. Telemachus steps forward boldly declaring that the beggar can do whatever he wishes. He sends his amazed mother to her quarters and instructs the swineherd to give Odysseus the bow. The doors are secretly bolted.*

Odysseus strings the bow easily. The hall falls ominously silent. He fires his first arrow perfectly through the twelve rings. Announcing that he will now hit another mark, Odysseus reveals himself and begins firing arrows at the suitors, killing Antinoos first. Panic ensues as the suitors quickly discover that their weapons have been locked away and they are trapped. An explosive barrage of arrows flies from Odysseus' bow and vengeful words erupt from his mouth. Eurymachos tries to blame Antinoos for the suitors' egregious behavior and pleads for Odysseus to spare his countrymen. When his pleading fails, he draws his sword and Odysseus shoots him dead. Telemachus kills another attacking suitor. Father and son fight side by side. Melanthios, the evil goatherd, climbs through vents into Odysseus' chambers returning with spears and armor. He goes again through the vents but this time Odysseus has sent men to ambush and capture him.

Athena, taking the form of Mentor, returns. She chastises Odysseus for having doubts, turns into a swallow perching high on a rafter, protects father and son against the suitors' spears, deranges their enemies' minds in fear and confusion, and watches as Odysseus and Telemachus slaughter the remaining suitors, killing one after another, sparing only the palace bard and herald at Telemachus' urging.

When the battle is over, Odysseus sends for his aged nurse to begun the cleanup. She raises a cry of triumph but Odysseus admonishes her, saying, "It is not piety to glory so over slain men" (Lattimore, 1999, p. 331). *He directs the staff to remove the bodies and clean the hall. He also instructs the nurse to bring forth all the disloyal maidservants for execution by hanging. Then they cut off the nose, ears, and genitals of the imprisoned Melanthios and feed them to the dogs. Odysseus orders the hall fumigated and cleansed with sulfur and warmly welcomes the remaining faithful servants.*

Interpretation. Odysseus cannot bear the humiliation he feels in this house of warrior ambitions. Humility feels too much like humiliation. Giving voice to his own haughty attitudes, the suitors' insults embarrass him repeatedly, for failure, weakness and inferiority are intolerable to the warrior mentality. But instead of reacting blindly, Odysseus plans to systematically eradicate each and every suitor, that is, each and every thought, value, and ambition that still imprison his love. This proverbial house cleaning need not involve literal killing; rather, it is the sword of honest and methodical self-examination employed by a maturing elder.

The contest Penelope devises is meant to remind Odysseus of another skill: the practice of raising consciousness. The discipline of bending and stringing the bow and holding it firm while sighting the target takes enormous practice. More to the point, it is highly mental - an internal discipline of balancing strength, timing, and experience. This contest is not a wife's manipulative test, a hoop Odysseus must jump through just to please her, like shooting Cupid's arrow; rather it symbolizes a profound gift from the feminine consciousness. When he takes up his bow, Odysseus rises to a higher level of consciousness. In firing his arrow perfectly through the ring heads, he demonstrates the Zen of archery – the complete unity of action, goal, and outcome. In a consciousness transcending thought and emotion, he acquires the level of consciousness necessary to eliminate destructive thought patterns.

Though no one else can bend and string Odysseus' bow, Telemachus comes close, suggesting that a son can achieve much of his father's power and skill, particularly as he grows into his own manhood. But Telemachus cannot heal his father. Only Odysseus can cleanse his own consciousness of his warrior fixations.

The ensuing battle Homer describes, however, is unbelievably violent – as violent as any movie or novel I know. For months, I struggled to understand this horrific scene of carnage and mayhem. More than just eradicating ego-driven greed and self-inflation, it was over-the-top brutal – a full-blown battle with all its myriad horrors. I asked myself, "What does this imagery mean? How can this slaughter be the act of a true elder?" Then, gradually, I understood: the scene is so massively horrifying because it reveals the size, scope, and nature of the violence embedded in the male psyche – all the personal wars a man has fought in his lifetime plus ten thousand years of warrior barbarism and aggression smoldering in the human psyche. Holocausts, ethnic cleansing, psychopathic dictators, and brutal wars continue to plague the world around us and Homer lays their cumulative horror at our feet.

This scene moves the action from the individual to the arche-typal, from personal soul-searching to a universal and collective confrontation with evil itself – the evil of crazed, out-of-control men. Odysseus, as Everyman, takes on this collective challenge when he agrees to transform himself. It is huge in this story because it is huge in reality. In this barbaric scene, we are witnessing what is inside men and what enlightened elders hope to transform in their own psyches. As universal hero, Odysseus' attempt to eliminate his own personal violence has lifted the lid of mankind's collective violence, just as he opened the pit into Hades, and it pours out of him. Interestingly, Odysseus eviscerates the genitals of his worst enemy, as if tacitly realizing the role testosterone from the testes plays in causing conflict, violence, and war.

Perhaps this scene might have been less violent. Could Odysseus have cleansed his warrior's psyche without such a bloodbath? Had the scene been sanitized, however, its powerful shock value, riveting our attention, would have been lost. Violence is the ultimate challenge humanity faces, and while many spiritual teachers have shown us better ways to deal with conflict (Jesus, Krishna, Buddha, Gandhi, Moses, Nanak), humanity as a whole has never come close to following their examples. The potential for violence dwells in all of us, for millennia of warfare created a powerful Darwinian selection for violence. Our collective work as aging men is to confront this primal evil and prevent it from being acted out in the world. As Cronus ate his young to hold onto power, it is often bitter old men who start wars.

Lest we assume that the suitors' masculine aggression is automatically "bad", we need to remind ourselves that great achievements in the world have also come from this same warrior orientation, but focused on conquering problems not each other. We will always need the capacity for intense and aggressive action; what must be transformed is the goal. The axes in Penelope's contest symbolize masculinity in both its constructive and destructive aspects – we can use an axe to kill or to build. We become a warrior not for our own sake, not just to be cool and powerful, but to serve something higher – the sacred value of life. The warriors in *The Iliad* never realized this purpose and fell into ten years of cyclical, foolish, and destructive violence. I believe *The Odyssey* was written to move us toward a consciousness beyond war.

Discussion. Unless a man recognizes and forcefully challenges the suitors of ambition, violence, and greed imprisoning his soul, he will fall under their spell again and again, even as he ages. He will envy other men, compete in the world of vanity and performance, and disparage himself when he fails. Each man needs to weed out the violent and competitive thoughts and fantasies that threaten to restore the hypnotic allure of the old way.

In reality, of course, sweeping clean the inner life of warrior habits is no simple task. For decades, warrior biology has coursed through our veins. Aroused by the scent and sight of competition and violence, real and symbolic, it activates the whole warrior complex – the power of the hunt, the boasting of comrades, the pride of uniforms and weapons, the sounds of battle, the call of war, and the imagined victory celebrations. A symphony of violence orchestrated by the entire culture locks us into the straitjacket of warrior rules, fantasies, and expectations. Biological, psychological, social and cultural, it's built into our nature, but elders, whose instinctual drives have diminished, will someday show us a way beyond war.

How do you "kill" aspirations for vanity, importance, wealth, and superiority in the male psyche? One method is to watch them come and go in meditation, learning how to release rather then pursue such thoughts. During actual upsets with others, one might practice a mantra like *Stop, Feel, Love*. Noticing emotional distress, *stop* identifying with the mind's grandiose and shame-filled thoughts and fantasies, *feel* the emotional arousal – sadness, unworthiness, inferiority, rage, whatever – and then release it, and then *love* – love the way things are, unconditionally, for love transforms everything. Using such a practice, the warrior drama we are imagining fades into the simple and beautiful light of day and we wake up to the present moment. We strive now to act consciously in the service of love, not war.

Remember, however, devious suitors will keep working at the edges of your awareness to stir up emotions and regain control of your mind and soul. They will whisper doubts, grandiose fantasies, and competitive promptings, hoping to reinstate the warrior thrill and setting us up for battle again. But, as Odysseus strung his bow with Zen-like awareness and fired through axe rings and suitors, elders can likewise focus their consciousness to eradicate one suitor-thought after another.

As I watch my own progress on this phase of the journey home, I have come to believe that leaving the war of compulsive accomplishment is not a one-time event but rather consists of a continuous process of self-correction. Giving up the goal orientation that defines masculinity is like dismantling a tall building

– if you are wise, you take it down one room, one floor, one step at a time. A one-day demolition, like sudden retirement, more often courts confusion, disorientation, and disaster. After a decade, I still fight the suitor battle. Faced with free time, I fall back into old productivity patterns, pursuing writing, computer tasks, or chores over relationships and love. The suitors sneak back into the castle of my psyche and urge me to go resume the fight. "Get busy!" they say. "You aren't doing anything worthwhile. You should be accomplishing important things." The battle is still going on because some part of me still fears that surrender equals death, failure, or unworthiness; yet every little victory over the suitors takes me home to love again and I wonder why I went back to the war. While we still need meaningful goals and projects in life – that is an integral part of personality, the trick is to find goals now that serve love, creativity, personal growth, and happiness, not power, money, ego, or productivity for its own sake.

The Challenge: Cleansing the Psyche. When you're ready, start to dismantle the tyranny of the warrior belief system. In the end, it didn't work for Agamemnon or Achilles, and it won't work for aging men. Come across the threshold of awakened consciousness into a new time of life. You cannot come home to love, passion, and purpose until you have left the war and defeated the powerful suitors controlling your heart and mind.

Growth Questions

1 Make a list of all the suitors that still hold your love prisoner (for example, secret desires for fame and fortune, competitive impulses triggered by other men, the vicarious thrills of TV sports). Which are the hardest to eradicate? Why?

2 When warrior ambitions, thoughts, and fantasies come to mind, can you simply observe each one, staying in pure

consciousness until it disappears? What happens when you succeed? What happens when you fail?

3 Spend the next three minutes practicing the mantra: Stop, Feel, and Love. Stop thinking, feel and release any emotions, and unconditionally love wherever you are. How does this practice change what you are doing in the moment?

4 Step back into the story as if it were your own dream. Be Odysseus, unleashing his rage at each and every suitor. How does that feel? What is really happening as you kill them one-by-one? Who are you really killing? How do you feel when they are all dead and gone? What kind of life do you want to create now?

The Story. *Eurykleia, Odysseus' old nurse, rushes up to Penelope's chambers. She tells Penelope of her husband's return and how he vanquished the suitors. At first, Penelope refuses to believe the old woman. Only when she mentions Odysseus' scar does Penelope's hope stir. She goes to the banquet hall to see for herself. She looks anew at the beggar but, despite her son's scolding, she sits quietly to study him in wonderment and uncertainty. She then conceives another test to determine if this beggar is really her husband. Meanwhile, Odysseus is growing concerned about the townspeople discovering his carnage and seeking revenge, so he instructs the palace staff to close and lock the hall and create festive party sounds to suggest that the long-expected wedding celebration is taking place.*

Odysseus bathes and puts on a regal tunic, and Athena magically enhances his stature and beauty. Sitting across from a still-reticent Penelope, Odysseus finally charges her with being stubborn and cold. She responds by instructing Eurykleia to move their bed outside her chamber into the hall. Penelope knows that the bed is so heavy, ponderous, and solid that no one could possible move it, least of all an old maidservant. This is her final test. Odysseus then confronts this ruse directly, for he knows everything about the bed - its size, weight, and elaborate construction – because he built it with his own hands. Recognizing the beggar knows facts only Odysseus could know, Penelope bursts into tears and a heartfelt reunion takes place. She confides her fear and distrust of men after suffering so many deceitful words and schemes from the suitors. Coming together now "at the threshold of old age" (Lattimore, 1999, p. 340), Odysseus and Penelope weep together.

Odysseus then tells Penelope that his trials are not yet over and recounts the words of the seer from Hades. Because the prophecy is ultimately positive, previewing a long life and happy old age, Penelope is not discouraged. The newly reconciled couple retires to their bedroom and they make love. Afterward, each tells the other about the years in between - the trials and tribulations they endured all these twenty years apart. Finally they fall asleep in each others' arms. The next morning, Odysseus announces he must visit Laertes, his elderly father.

Interpretation. At long last, Odysseus is truly home, both physically and psychologically. He and Penelope join together in authentic loving and Odysseus resumes his true identity and rightful place in the family and community, though now embracing the transforming wisdom of age and experience.

Odysseus and Penelope reconcile in a mature, honest, and age-appropriate way. He gives her time to get used to his presence, test and reveal his true identity, and grow comfortable and familiar with him again. Penelope finally drops her guard and accepts her husband with open arms. With her fear and distrust resolved, they make love and then stay up late into the night to share their separate stories with honesty, patience, completeness, and vulnerability. Relieved, relaxed and exhausted, they fall asleep together, merging into the healing unity of love.

Discussion. Men need to know that good intentions are not enough to come home. They must put down sword and shield and open to real, imperfect, and vulnerable love. Some, having never worked through their own Circe issues, were never fully in the relationship in the first place; others joined the family only sporadically. There is so much ground to cover. Coming home to love, therefore, asks for a mature sharing of the wounds each has experienced through this long, complicated, sometimes painful and usually unintended, separation.

The process of reconciliation can actually stumble along for years with many ups and downs. With a history of problems and disappointments, many couples lack the relationship experience, faith, and communication ability needed to reconcile and simply return to co-existence again. We cannot idealize this process because it is imperfect and difficult, nor should we minimize the requisite skills – skills of patience, communication, and insight into our interacting vulnerabilities. Our culture needs an under-standing of this stage of marriage, facilitated by new healing methods, sacred rituals, and community support. In their absence, perhaps you and your mate will have the courage to experiment and share what you have learned.

For me, relationship in the third age is an ongoing experiment in personal growth – my becoming more me, my wife becoming more her, and the kids and grandkids becoming more who they are as well, and relating from this new growth. It's about individ-uation, respect and love. For me, it is only when I am truly myself that I can be truly close, otherwise I am merely adjusting my persona to fit the circumstances. We are, in effect, meeting again for the first time, revealing new parts of the self and personality, along with changing values and needs, that had no time to develop in the busy middle years. Like Odysseus and Penelope, we are looking at each other anew to see who this person is now. As this renewed sharing takes place, real intimacy opens. Fortunately there is usually plenty of time and oppor-tunity in the aging years to work on this rapprochement. We will also come to depend on each other in new ways during these years as time and decline follow their prescribed course, and, in the process, see into each other's souls in ways never expected. A gift, a grace, sometimes a heavy burden – in maturity we may also come to experience this final journey as sacred.

The Challenge: Returning to Love. Explain your heartfelt desire for genuine and loving intimacy but don't rush reconciliation. You may be rediscovering this depth of intimacy for the first time in decades – both of you need time to develop trust and unlock your heart. Be responsible for your own reactivity to prevent it from triggering old conflict patterns. Be gentle and forgiving. Tell the stories of your lives – there is much you haven't shared even if the "facts" are known. Trust, hope, experiment, pray, play, talk, and keep trying. Understanding and accepting this process will help you find your own path back to each other. If your intentions are good, Athena – your own higher self – will help you along.

Growth Questions

1 How might you create a safe and supportive encounter with your spouse and family? Can you be patient and appreciate that many encounters, verbal and otherwise, may be necessary for trust and love to heal?

2 What will be the most difficult feelings and experiences to share with your spouse? What will be the most difficult feelings and experiences to hear from her?

3 Can you resist becoming defensive in this sharing? Can you acknowledge the mistakes you made with compassion for yourself and for her?

4 Step back into the story as if it were your own dream. Be Odysseus sharing this long story of foolish mistakes, heartaches, and longing. Be Penelope dealing with old feelings of anger, betrayal and, most deeply, unrequited love. Make love with the hunger of twenty years. Be there for each other.

Chapter 6

Final Challenges

Although Odysseus has reunited with son, wife, and home, he is not finished with his changes. Now he must also come to terms with old age, take a stand for permanent peace in his psyche, and complete the ritual prescribed by Teiresias - finding a home in the divine.

The Story. *Hermes conducts the souls of the dead suitors to Hades. Before they arrive in Hades, Achilles, Agamemnon, and several other souls are discussing their own deaths. Agamemnon in particular feels cheated, believing Achilles died a hero's death in Troy while he died ignobly at the hands of his scheming wife. More importantly, they seem implicitly to realize that vanity and revenge stole their lives – not such a great boon after all. In the midst of this conversation, Hermes and the deceased suitors arrive and the suitors are asked how they died. The suitors describe their slaughter in detail, complaining that Odysseus had the unfair advantage of a god's assistance. Agamemnon, however, praises Odysseus' success and again laments his own pitiful demise.*

Meanwhile, accompanied by the oxherd, the swineherd, and his son, Odysseus travels to his father's home, and observes its well-maintained and abundant orchards. Odysseus at first believes his father must be the poor servant of another because he is dressed in rags and works at labor. Odysseus greets his father and pretends to be an old friend of his long-lost son. Laertes immediately breaks down in grief-filled tears, pouring dirt over his own face and head in a display of terrible sorrow, and provoking Odysseus to reveal his true identity. Laertes, too, asks for proof of identity and Odysseus once again reveals the scar sustained from his childhood wild boar attack. He also recalls happy times with his father in their gardens. Another weeping reunion takes place and Telemachus and the others join them in Laertes' home to celebrate. They bathe and dress, and Athena renders Laertes handsome again. Another old and devoted servant and his sons are warmly received as well. All share a festive and happy dinner.

Interpretation. The souls of the dead complain bitterly of their fate, suggesting that hanging onto old identities and issues only creates more suffering. The deceased suitors represent the inflated ego's final grumblings that having to surrender its glorious warrior destiny is too hard or unfair. Homer pays little attention to such whining – the path of real growth lies ahead.

Once he finds his father, Odysseus mistakes the dirty clothes of a devoted gardener for the state of destitution. Though he may look impoverished, and surely misses his son, Laertes is actually doing very well. He cares lovingly for his thriving orchards, supporting life, beauty, and the future. The garden metaphor refers to the way a man gathers the fruits of his life in its final season. He discovers which seeds have blossomed and which have not – a harvest that no man can really predict. Laertes also cares for the *Garden,* the holy ground of human existence, which the awakened elder finds in old age when the imminence of death heightens his awareness of the Earth's beauty and abundant grace. Though grieving his lost son, Laertes has made a healthy adjustment to old age. The other elder in the scene is also functioning well in his service to Laertes. Together they remind us that aging is not about money or clothes but the connection to life, meaningful work, and love of family.

This part of the story finds the male lineage healing – grandfather, son, and grandson – restoring an archetypal order in the psyche previously torn apart by war.

Discussion. Odysseus is beginning now to contemplate the stages of aging he will face – the "young" old of reasonable health and activity, the "middle" old of downward adjustments while maintaining independence, and the "old" old of failing health and preparing for death – and the unique purpose, value, and gifts they involve. The first stage opens consciousness to the reality of aging, inviting reflection, preparation, and "bucket-lists", but little changes in everyday issues and activities. As bodies age and death becomes more real or easily imagined, the second stage offers us the various roles of elders – teaching, caring and serving, along with the personal wisdom that life is precious. In the third stage, approaching our own dying, we gracefully surrender back into the ground of creation – if we have become wise.

Still in the first stage of aging, Odysseus watches his father, observing his changed values, his well-tended "garden", and the fruits of wisdom and consciousness that now blossom in the movement from second to third stages. Laertes has completed the reminiscing task of age, cares deeply for life, and dwells in closer unity with all of Creation. This time can be a wondrous, humbling, grace-filled meditation filled with surprises, gratitude, and wisdom – if we can avoid being critical of our present living conditions and appreciate instead the continuing miracle of life.

We often think that the trials and losses of aging are unfair, too much to bear, and only negative. But there are hidden gifts in every loss. One friend underwent two cancer surgeries. It was an awful time for him. Later, however, he told me, "People praise me for my courage – to live through cancer in 2004, and now through jaw surgery and recovery in 2011. But I just think of it as my life. In some ways I've never been happier – writing short pieces for my weekly Writing Workshop. I am very introverted but I have my wife and her children to take care of me and love me. I just feel blessed. Blessed that I have the capacity to read your manuscript, and that you have called me to do so. My challenge seems to be to get out of myself, away from my computer, out of my office. My wife is always asking me to spend more time with her; more meaningful time. As I write this it seems like I'm being offered a huge gift." I could not have said it better.

The Challenge: Accepting Old Age. Aging is not what we think. What appears on the outside – old bodies, old faces, and old clothes, hides a natural but profoundly meaningful process taking us along a consciousness-transforming path. Our inner evolution will bring a deep understanding of our life, prepare us for death, and awaken intuitions of what comes next – if we explore this unfolding process with interest, awareness, and compassion.

Growth Questions

1 What grew in your garden? How do you appreciate the expected and unexpected blossoms of your life? Are you still grumbling about past failures instead of being present to new wonders?
2 How have you made peace with your father and his aging? What was his aging like and what did you learn from it?
3 What kind of meaningful work do you do now? How do you care for the garden of life as you age?
4 Step back into the story as if it were your own dream. Feel the shock of witnessing old age and then the discovery that it is not so awful. Be Telemachus who now notices your aging. Sense the mystery of Earth as an old man and how differently you view life now. This part of the dream holds so much implicit wisdom on the aging process.

The Story. *Despite his heart-warming reunion with his father, Odysseus fears the approach of the suitors' families intent on avenging their deaths. The messenger, Rumor, has been spreading news of their slaughter throughout the city and, in spite of cautionary words from an aged warrior, half the gathered assembly work themselves up into a frenzied rage and rush out in pursuit of Odysseus. Athena speeds to*

Zeus for help. He advises her to appeal to both sides, seeking peace-making oaths, forgiveness of deaths, and resumption of old friendships. Warned of their avengers' approach, Odysseus, Telemachus, Laertes and the old servant immediately prepare for battle. As the fighting begins, Laertes, with Athena's assistance, kills the father of Antinoos, one of the most evil suitors.

As emotions intensify, Zeus throws down a great thunderbolt and Athena cries, "Hold back, men of Ithaca, from the wearisome fighting, so that most soon, and without blood, you can settle everything" (Lattimore, 1999, p. 359). Terrified of Zeus' power, the suitors and relatives turn to flee. Athena advises Odysseus to cease fighting or face Zeus' wrath. The battle ends with pledges of peace sworn by all, a process skillfully directed by Athena once again disguised as Mentor.

Interpretation. A man cannot come home if he is easily drawn back into the fires of male aggression. A family and community cannot heal if residual hatreds are nursed. Zeus, the highest god, draws the line – it's time for peace. Laertes demonstrates that elders can still, on occasion, be fierce and strong, and, as if serving Karma, he completes the destruction of the evil and greedy Antinoos lineage.

But it takes the wrath of Zeus to end this generations-long cycle of violence. Someone with great authority has to intervene. It's as if Odysseus' higher self, observing his rush to battle, pulls rank – the archetypal conscience of a god declaring an end to foolishness. This kind of stance is the prerogative and responsibility of the mature elder who can step into the fray of youthful warriors and say, with the authority of a god, "Enough! You are better than this. Be responsible men not adolescent boys. Grow up."

Discussion. Old men are not fit for war. While they can still be angry and froth at the mouth, aging bodies are not fit for the fight nor do old men really want to resume the war. Their proper role now is the mature voice of conscience, taking stands on issues of importance to life. If middle-aged men are responsible for initiating youth into responsible masculinity, old men are responsible for initiating society toward love, decency, and other higher purposes.

Older men in western society have failed profoundly in this area, for the culture has largely forgotten this wisdom role, and therefore so have we. An aging man's desire for new meaning and purpose holds this secret longing – to serve as a voice of wisdom and peace. One of the tasks of aging men is to foster this potential in each other and the result, as we will see, may be a new fusion of love and work in the final stage of life.

As I age, I have less and less tolerance for the futility and foolishness of war and its endless sublimations. I understand young men, as I was once, need to feel the natural fierceness erupting from their biology, but we can encourage its expression toward so many positive and constructive ends. Old men should never manipulate the young men's warrior energy to serve their own ends – an example of real evil – we are here to heal and serve peace. My generation searches for ways to share this hard-won wisdom.

The Challenge: Choosing Peace. Make peace. Put life first. Take a stand for civility, kindness, and truth. Help build a society based on mature oaths, genuine forgiveness, and meaningful relationships. The role of elder bequeaths this greater responsibility to aging men.

Growth Questions

1 Have you been drawn into old battles in your aging years, battles that you could instead forgive and put to rest? With whom? How might you put down the sword and make peace?

2 What recent event has the ring of Zeus' thunderbolt anger,

carrying the message that enough is enough?

3   Which parts of your community need confronting, healing, and restoration? What might your role be in this healing?

4   Step back into the story as if it were your own dream. Feel yourself beingdrawn back into war. Be Zeus and throw the thunderbolt of "Enough!" down to Earth. Become Athena, disguised as Mentor, negotiating oaths of peace for the sake of future generations.

The Story. *In Hades long ago, the prophet Teiresias gave Odysseus a profound but cryptic prophecy. He was told that, upon returning home and restoring his kingdom, he was to travel with an oar through many cities until he came to a country where no men knew of the sea, ships, or oars, nor do they use salt in their food. Odysseus would recognize this destination when he meets someone who mistakes his oar for a winnowing fan. On that spot, he should plant the oar in the ground and sacrifice a ram, a bull, and a boar to Poseidon. He was then to return home and offer hecatombs – the sacrifice of one hundred cattle – to the full pantheon of gods one at a time. The seer added that Odysseus would then live into a ripe and peaceful old age with death coming gently from the sea.*

Interpretation. What can this strange prophecy mean and how might it complete our hero's psychological and spiritual transformation? *The Odyssey* ends before we learn whether Odysseus fulfills this mysterious destiny. Examining the prophecy symbolically, however, we begin see something of its deeper import.

The oar Odysseus carries is a symbol of masculine power, the human power that drives ships when the winds are slack or blowing the wrong way. Carried far from the sea, however, the oar's original purpose is surrendered – it has no such power inland. But there it may become a winnowing fan, suggesting an altogether different purpose. An early farm implement, the winnowing fan was used to separate wheat from chaff. As a symbol, its function describes the process of discrimination – the ability to separate seeds from husks, what is important from what is not, the essence from the superficial. Moreover, one of the spiritual goals of discriminating the important from the unimportant is to distinguish consciousness from its contents, that is, pure and thought-free awareness from the constant flow of words, ideas, beliefs, goals, perceptions, feelings, and actions. In pure consciousness, we awaken from the dominance of mind forms in general and reactive masculinity in particular. We open into the consciousness of the universe.

Odysseus' three sacrifices represent the ritual surrender of his biologically-driven male energies of sex and aggression. In other words, he must relinquish his masculine instincts to achieve this next stage of consciousness. That he must make this sacrifice to Poseidon, the god of the deep whom he insulted and whose son he blinded, is no accident. If Poseidon symbolizes the psyche's earliest terror, the "father" of all trauma, then this sacrifice represents both the *recognition* of terror as a force that once drove his violence, and its ritual *surrender* as step toward further psychological transformation. Furthermore, Poseidon as a denizen of the salty sea, may also symbolize "blood, sweat and tears" - the primordial substance of life itself that spills in acts of violence.

In offering hecatombs, Odysseus personally encounters the divine in each of its many facets. Like the Hindus, the polytheistic Greeks refracted divinity into a pantheon of individual gods, each reflecting some quality or aspect of the human experience of itself and divinity. As you become what you dwell upon, at least temporally, so Odysseus absorbs the divine in each meeting. In the process, he is steadily transforming himself.

In summary, the seer has given Odysseus a ritual for honoring and integrating the great transformation achieved during his long and arduous journey home – his shift from biological and aggressive masculinity to awakened spiritual consciousness.

Traveling inland, he leaves the maritime battles of the masculine ego for an inner journey, one taking him to the direct awareness of divinity. Homer is suggesting that this may be the ultimate task of aging men; he puts it in the future because very few yet recognize or realize its potential. If this final journey goes well, it opens into a new land – the land of the Self – where ego, self, soul, world, and divinity are one.

Discussion. An interesting contrast of aging men can be found in the tales of two legendary college coaches. John Wooden, the UCLA basketball coach, retired at 64 and moved quietly into private life, turned inward, and then in his 80's returned to the world speaking sagely about the lessons of his career. He died shortly before his 100th birthday. Penn State football coach, Joe Paterno, on the other hand, continued coaching until 85 when the horrific sexual behavior of his assistant, which he had known about for years, exploded in scandal. Confused and vaguely regretful, Paterno died suddenly as the shocking extent of this horror came to light.

Like Wooden, Odysseus went in search of the meaning of his life, returning home as a wise and humble elder. Paterno did not look inward, never left the war of college football, and like the mythic Cronus, ended up sacrificing numerous children to a known predator. These contrasting stories, like a morality play, illustrate the incredible importance of understanding the tasks and challenges of aging. We will not, as men, realize the full potential of age if we refuse to leave the war. In the journey of aging, men become open doors of wisdom and spirituality, bringing new light into the world.

This final journey inward has, at times, been difficult for me. I struggle with feelings of futility caused by several realizations: That nearly everyone's life work is quickly forgotten in the frantic free-for-all of "modern" culture, that in reality we each have so little impact on the foolishness of war and humankind's degradation of the Earth and its creatures, that all I came to personally understand about life will disintegrate like dust in death, and that each generation will make so many of the same mistakes. Reminding myself of the winnowing fan, however, I move from content to consciousness and joy springs anew. For me, the world is reborn as sacred in awakened consciousness and all these questions suddenly cease to matter unless, like the suitors, they sneak up on me again. This movement into thought-free consciousness is the enlightenment shift the mystics have always spoken of. With the natural decline of testosterone, aging is the time to make it. This is one of the gifts of the elder's journey home and each of us will find our own way to experience it.

The Challenge: Finding Holy Ground. Surrendering biological masculinity for spiritual maturity, we are called to travel this final leg of the journey inward to the divine center of Self. Ultimately, it is a merging of consciousness and being into divine union, a merging that anticipates the ultimate transformation of death. In old age, this oneness can be experienced as life itself, which is why life becomes so sacred to the old.

Growth Questions

1 Are you moving more deeply into your interior, into the deep self, as you age? What are you noticing?

2 In some ancient cultures, elder rituals helped men shift from warriors to elders. What kind of ritual might allow you to surrender instinctual masculinity for the elder's spiritual consciousness? Could you create your own ritual?

3 How do you surrender to the divine? How does this surrender kindle the energies of peace and love?

4 Step back into the story as if it were your own dream. Travel to this strange land with your oar. Plant it in the ground and use your powers of discrimination to shift from thought to consciousness itself. Then sacrifice your

masculine powers in recognition of the fear that once drove them. How do you feel? Then make a sacrifice to every god individually, seeing in each a part of your own nature. One hundred times! How are you being changed by this ritual?

Chapter 7

Review and Final Lessons

Following Odysseus' adventures through eighteen profound challenges of aging, we have shared a long and soulful journey from middle-aged warrior to the awakened elder. The more deeply we live this road of trials and transformations, the more deeply we realize the tremendous growth potential of aging, and the equally tremendous cost of ignoring it. Before we explore how men can help each other succeed on this journey, let's stop for a moment and retrace our steps. The journey's eighteen challenges can be summed up as follows:

Eighteen Challenges Men Face Coming Home
From the War

Early Mistakes
Repeating the Past – Raid on the Cicones
Falling Asleep – Land of the Lotus-Eaters
Loathing the Self – Island of the Cyclops
Demanding Extreme Self-Sufficiency – King of the Winds
Turning Against the Self – Island of the Laestrygonians

Transformational Experiences
Coming to Terms with the Feminine – Circe the Witch
Facing Death – Descent into Hades
Resisting Illusions – Call of the Sirens
Moving Through Fear and Depression – Skylla and Charybdis
Stumbling on Divinity – The Island of Thrinakia

Homecoming
Saying Goodbye to the Goddess – Leaving Calypso
Celebrating Home – Feast of the Phaeacians
Preparing for Homecoming – Ithaca at Last
Cleansing the Psyche – Confronting the Suitors
Returning to Love – Reunion with Penelope

Final Challenges
Accepting Old Age – Visit with Laertes
Choosing Peace, Ending War – "Stop This Quarrel!"
Finding Holy Ground – Ritual for the Gods

Reviewing Odysseus' eighteen challenges, we see that they tell a single story of coming home from the long war of adulthood. Leaving the war, we often make the mistake of continuing to battle in all we do, or fall asleep in time-wasting activities. Then, when we do turn inward, we often don't like what we find, push the immature self away with ridicule and distain, resume our customary heroic self-sufficiency, and when all this fails, run from our own self-hatred. So it is that Everyman makes every mistake. Things begin to change, however, when we meet the feminine within; that is, when we open to the energies of love.

Because our love will be directed to real women when we get home, the feminine calls us to face our hidden fears of intimacy and rework our relationship expectations – a continuous challenge on the way home. Things change further when she asks us to look at death. We will die. All before us have died. All following us will die. This transformational encounter with death prompts a profound reappraisal of our past behavior and deepest values, and brings us in touch with the many seductive illusions that maintain the fantasy of immortality. As we resist our illusions, we unearth the fear and depression that has empowered them. Then, sooner or later, we will surrender everything – identity, beliefs, attachments, and material security.

Interestingly, all these steps coincide with the universal spiritual path.

The good news is that the progressive maturation of self and consciousness leads back to love – authentic love, not fantasy idealizations. We return to a mortal and to an imperfect relationship, but once this reality is clear, we are almost there. Happiness, denied for decades, bursts in celebration. We need to approach home carefully, however, for one of the final barriers is the ego's myriad ambitions that still hold love prisoner. We must confront these persistent suitors of the soul with the sincere and unsentimental sword of truth. Then, finally, we find love. It is an older, more mature love, and we begin to understand the real nature of aging, the critical choice of peace, and the importance of reconciling with the divine.

We might also recap the lessons of Odysseus' journey with this abbreviated summary:

1 Don't repeat the past – you've done that enough.
2 Don't just go to sleep.
3 Instead, get in touch with your real self without judgment.
4 Remember, more heroic self-sufficiency is not growth.
5 Neither is self-hatred.
6 Instead open to the feminine qualities of love that dwell in your heart.
7 Understand the meaning and purpose of death – especially your own.
8 Resist the illusions that maintain your fantasy of an endless future.
9 Face the fear and depression underlying these illusions.
10 Prepare to let go of material security for the sake of transformation.
11 Surrender the expectation of perfection in human relationships.

12 Be happy, you're almost home.
13 On arriving, be humble, perceptive, and plan well.
14 Eradicate the many "warrior" motives that still imprison your love.
15 Be sensitive and patient in your homecoming reunion.
16 Understand and accept the gifts of old age.
17 Find peace and forgiveness with your family and community.
18 Experience the sacred nature of all life.

We can see a steady line of psychological and spiritual growth here. The first five challenges ask a man to face the central problem – himself. The next five offer a remedy for that problem – a set of transformational experiences that progressively dissolve his egocentric male reactivity into an awakened consciousness that spiritual teachers from all traditions would approve. The next five challenges bring the traveler home at last, his psychological and spiritual transformation paving the way for real and meaningful love. In the final three challenges, he makes peace with old age, the world, and divinity, opening a potential new stage of life.

I should point out that these eighteen challenges do not comprise a checklist – items to read, perform, and dismiss – nor do they comprise a necessary sequence, to be completed only in the order listed. In reality, we work on each of these challenges over and over, gradually moving down the list, sometimes skipping ahead, sometimes dropping back. Like the children's board game "Chutes and Ladders", we get ahead, slide back, and climb up again. In fact, aging is messy and Odysseus gets knocked around a lot. He repeats the same mistakes, trips over his arrogance again and again, and is endlessly defeated. While his experiences are all in the service of psychological and spiritual growth, they are often not very pretty. But unless he chooses to go forward and keep learning, his growth will stop.

And so it is with each of us.

Suffering and Joy. Throughout his long journey home, Odysseus suffers. We hear him and his men crying openly, deeply, with great anguish and often with hopelessness. Still they get up every day and move on. For ten years! Aging has this kind of challenge in it. I don't personally know any one who has "lived happily ever after". There is simply too much to lose, too much to go wrong, and then, of course, you die. People don't talk a lot about this, but it's real.

In the face of pain and suffering, men want to solve the problem of aging and death, but it cannot be solved. They want to reduce it to tasks that can be mastered, but it cannot be mastered. Aging is a conundrum that defeats the ego. Instead we need to learn how to adapt to this new world of aging, to let go of the hero, and open into the consciousness of love in whatever happens. One man explained to me that his mantra in old age is "accept, forgive, and love", a mantra that transforms his suffering into growth.

But Odysseus also experiences joy and love. His sojourns with Circe and Calypso, his visit with the Phaeacians, his reunions with Telemachus, Laertes and Penelope, are all times of gratitude, rejoicing, and love. The journey of aging is potentially filled with joy if we pursue growth and love with sincerity. Had Odysseus remained in the Land of the Lotus-Eaters, he might not have suffered so obviously, but he would not have found love and joy. Though aging is a bumpy ride, joy follows pain as certainly as day follows night if we can learn to live awakened consciousness. Paradoxically, pain is the cost of hanging on to the past but we each learn this slowly, often against our will. In letting go of resistance, we resume the journey and find our way home.

The Physical Challenges of Aging. Part of the suffering of age is physical – the symptoms, illnesses, and accidents that accompany failing health, so where are aging's physical challenges in this great story? While Laertes offers us one example of the declining powers of old age, his is a portrayal of adjustment, acceptance, and responsibility. We don't hear much about the negative side of physical aging, or do we?

Reminding ourselves that this is a *symbolic* story, we need look no further than Odysseus's crew, ships, and raft for physical symbols of strength, stature, and wellbeing. They represent his "body" – solid, dependable, and confident. As the story proceeds, however, Poseidon and Zeus steadily decimate his physical strength and stature. By the time Odysseus reaches the Phaeacians, he has lost everything save his actual body. Isn't that what we experience in aging? But we arrive home in *good enough* shape to complete the work of aging. Remember, the battle Odysseus fights with the suitors is psychological, not literal, and it's within, not out in the "real" world. As long as we can think, imagine, feel and speak, illness, or decrepitude need not abort the journey home. Which leads next to the importance of passion.

The Power of Passion. Throughout his long and arduous journey, Odysseus' passion to come home constantly drives him onward. Surviving obstacle after obstacle, trial after trial, never giving up, he always moves forward. This is the passion we need to confront aging with integrity and to make the journey worth the suffering.

What passion moves you forward? What value, vision, person, or purpose calls you into the day and into your life even at those times when you feel lost, wounded, or discouraged? What imperative matters so much that surrendering it would erase your will to live? This question of passion is critical for without it, obstacles become insurmountable, and pain becomes suffering. Why even try to go home if home means nothing to you?

Passion, of course, comes in endless shapes and sizes. It might involve building model trains, listening to great symphonies, reading poetry, taking photographs, helping grandchildren, cultivating flowers, or writing your memoirs. Whatever it is, try to get inside it – look for its personal meaning, purpose, and energy, for real passion generates real growth. Indeed, passion encourages and sometimes even forces growth, and aging is nothing if not profound growth. Passion is the drive of the plant to reach its full beauty; the press of the individuating self to break through the tarmac of old beliefs and habits; and the ripening of the soul and its gifts for a new season of expression. And when one passion ends, wait for a new one to emerge. Passion, like life itself, springs forth at every stage for every stage brings the possibilities of growth. Odysseus was driven by passion and was richer by far for following it. The men who age most successfully don't have fewer problems, they have more passion.

Sigmund Freud taught us that the two fundamental values in life are love and work. If we age meaningfully, love and work come together in the creation of new passions. We now love through work. And, rather than giving up the warrior stance, we use our warrior skills and resources now in the service of the heart. It is no longer about being the alpha male or the top dog, it's about loving, and the opportunities to love come often – a disabled spouse, a dying friend, a community project, a grandchild's homework assignment, or baseball game.

In this growing capacity for love, a man may rediscover *soul work* – his own unique *charisma*. A Greek word, charisma is often translated as "gift of grace" or "divinely conferred talent". This gift already lies hidden in a man's heart. It is, in fact, central to his nature, so present that he often overlooks it or takes it for granted. *Who we are most deeply is our gift,* one that only needs recognizing and nourishing to flower. We may express our charisma in any number of ways; the key is that the way we express it makes us feel happy, connected, hopeful, inspired, and generous. It is one of the most important reasons we came here. We'll say more about passion later on.

Is Odysseus Old Enough to be Considered Old? From what we know of Odysseus – the fact that he has a twenty-year-old son and no grandchildren, one might argue that he is not old enough to be doing the work of aging yet. I would guess that his age was between 45 and 50 years old. Does this age range discount all we have learned about aging so far?

Forty-five probably represented the beginning of old age in ancient Greece, for thirty was the expected life span at that time (though if one made it past the age of five, the odds of reaching 45 increased greatly). Of course some men, like Laertes, lived to a ripe old age, but few were so fortunate. It would be fair to say, therefore, that Odysseus is just crossing the threshold into old age in this tale – what gerontologists call the "young old" – a good time to be preparing for the challenges of aging.

Odysseus has also not yet encountered the miracle of grand-children, an opportunity that invigorates so many aging men. This omission compromises the story some, for the next gener-ation symbolizes new life, hope for the future, and another chance to contribute meaningfully before we die. If I were writing this story, I would give Odysseus two or three grand-children and picture him entertaining them with exciting stories of his adventures and pretend sword fights (though never glori-fying violence and killing). I would also have him contributing to their adolescent growth, encouraging heroic strivings toward the expression of their gifts – ego serving society – rather than the development of a warrior complex for its own sake or its owner's grandiosity.

Does this absence of grandchildren negate the teaching value of our story? Of course not, it just leaves out a page or two. But imaging Odysseus' new role with his grandchildren opens up so many possibilities. What would you like to see him doing with them? What do you love to do most with your grandchildren?

Odysseus' Kingdom. Odysseus was a king. He had wealth, land, servants, and status. As few of us are kings or wealthy, how does this story apply to our lives? The answer depends on how you look at wealth.

In aging, we finally discover that wealth is not material; rather it is found in family, community, and spirit. We may have espoused this value before, but now we know it is indeed true. Material wealth alone will not make us happy. Restoring our own "kingdom", therefore, means restoring love not splendor. Poverty is not only about money, it is about isolation, loneliness and depression. We find our true wealth in relationship.

Growth Questions

1 How does your journey compare to the stages and challenges of Odysseus adventures? Where are you on the journey and what have your learned so far?

2 Do you feel the passion to come home? What is so priceless in your life that you would rather die than lose it?

3 Where is your kingdom? What do you most want to find there?

4 Step back into the story as if it were your own dream. Which challenge feels the most unfinished for you? Return to it, resume the action, and struggle with the problem seeking new insights. Play it out in new ways. What does it bring to mind? What are you really trying to do?

Chapter 8

Spiritual Realizations

The Odyssey is not only a psychologically deep and meaningful psychological story; it depicts Odysseus' spiritual evolution as guided by Zeus and his agents. As the most powerful Greek god, Zeus represents the spiritual force behind this epic, though Athena and various lesser spiritual figures accomplish the day-to-day spiritual guidance. The whole story is deeply spiritual, and as an archetypal narrative, it tells the story of our collective departure from and return to the sacred.

The tale begins in Zeus' garden with the wedding of a goddess and a mortal – a symbol of the universally prophesized divinization of human life. Warring egos, however, drive the hero out of paradise and he pursues his own ego-inflating ends through competition, conquest, and war until the whole adventure grows wearisome and meaningless. Then, like the Prodigal Son, the hero's goal is to find his way home, which spiritually speaking, means, returning to the divine.

Zeus intervenes three times in this journey – first, authorizing Odysseus's escape from Calypso's island to prompt his journey onward; second, punishing Odysseus for violating the divine terms of Hyperion's realm – like Karma, divine law always exacts a price when ego betrays divinity; and third, demanding a final end to the war in order to move the story toward its spiritual conclusion, which lies hidden in the seer's strange prophecy.

The Blind Seer's Prophecy – Final Challenges

Though we previously examined part of the spiritual signifi-cance of the blind seer's prophecy. I would suggest that it holds two further spiritual possibilities (bringing the number of challenges to five in the fourth chapter in balance with the three previous chapters – a nice symmetry). The additional challenges are *Divinizing Humanity* and *Finding Heaven Here.*

Divinizing Humanity. If we understand that Zeus is part of each person reading this story, we begin to realize that we, too, are part of the divine acting to change ourselves. This change, however, comes not through Zeus' direct action, but through the subtle influence of his main appointed agent, Athena, the divine feminine.

Athena accompanies Odysseus every step of the way, often shape-shifting into others to move the plot along. As a symbol of his own feminine side, she guides him with whispered intuitions, transformative experiences, and direct instruction. Eventually Athena's influence reunites Odysseus and Penelope in a renewed chemistry of love, after which he pursues his ultimate spiritual quest. In essence, Athena represents the undeveloped love in a man leading him to the sacred marriage of the mortal masculine and the divine feminine, a merging that gradually divinizes the ego.

In the final unfinished chapter of the story, Odysseus is instructed to complete a ritual prescribed by the blind seer, a ritual that involves making sincere offerings to every significant god and goddess in the Greek pantheon, that is, to every form of the divine. Since you become what you meditate on, at least during the meditation, so do you merge with divine when you focus exclusively on it. Because each god symbolizes a human quality or dimension in divine form, he is progressively divinizing every corresponding aspect in his own nature. In other words, he is merging humanity with divinity in himself to give birth to a new kind of man.

In like fashion, each man is ultimately called to incarnate the divine through the sacred marriage of mortal masculinity and divine femininity. The symbols of this marriage can be found in the ultimate dualities of all mythologies – it is the sacred union of sky and Earth, spirit and matter, Samara and Nirvana, Shiva and Shakti, mind and thought, sacred and profane, particle and wave, consciousness and contents. A corresponding process, of course, happens for women. The resulting divine birth, however, is not a sudden, once-and-for-all event. It is, rather, a gradual process of integration, transformation, and divinization - an ongoing metamorphosis toward a mystical state of awareness.

In merging with the divine feminine, men gradually become agents of divine love. In the process, we are also creating a new understanding of God. In spiritual development, we first conceive the divine but place it outside ourselves. Next we experience the divine as everywhere but omit ourselves. Then we begin to realize that everywhere means us, too, and we learn to experience our consciousness as divine consciousness and our being as divine being, creating a divine union in each of us. In this way, a new kind of human arises in the world.

Finding Heaven Here. The Jungian author Helen Luke, in her lovely book *Old Age: Journey into Simplicity* written at the age of eighty-three, talks of this union with divinity and how it leads to the divinization of the world itself. After writing her own version of the unfinished chapter of the seer's prophecy, Luke explains, "It is a return to the same simplicity and oneness with nature and spirit that these people here have (referring to the inland people in her story that Odysseus eventually meets), but they live without understanding, as do beast and flower. In the Return, however, the oneness is known, experienced, through the awakening of the mind of God in each man and woman. That future now becomes possible for you, my friend" (Luke, 1987, p.20). Similarly, Thomas Falkner, in his chapter, "Homeric Heroism, Old Age, and the End of the Odyssey", writes, "The inland journey thus become a final farewell to the heroic age and a passage to the peaceable kingdom" (Falkner, 1989, p. 53).

This oneness with nature and spirit brings us to the final

spiritual challenge: Finding Heaven here. The mystics have told us for centuries that the experience of divinity leads to the experience of the divine world all around us (Robinson, 2009). When we finally experience everything as divinity, we enter the Heaven on Earth and the divinization of the material universe is complete.

As a cultural dream, *The Odyssey* envisions a profound cultural change that can bring humankind home from the war. Many will resist this awakening and wars will continue as long as ego and instinct dominate the world. Aging, however, offers a uniquely valuable opportunity for profound psychological and spiritual change through three dynamic processes: *initiation, transformation,* and *revelation* (Robinson, 2012). Encounters with loss, love, and death initiate us to a new stage of spiritual development, dissolving illusions, transforming self and consciousness, and revealing a sacred universe all around us.

In the Gospel of Thomas, Jesus tells us, "When you make the two into one, and when you make the inner like the outer and the outer like the inner, and the upper like the lower, and when you make male and female into a single one, so that the male will not be male nor the female be female, when you make eyes in place of an eye, a hand in place of a hand, a foot in place of a foot, an image in place of an image, then you will enter the Kingdom" (Gospel of Thomas, 22). In this merging of human and divine, of mortal and sacred, a profound transformation occurs revealing the divine world.

Discussion. This universal story of being born into a divine world, losing it, and searching for it again, of which *The Odyssey* is one of countless examples, has also been my own story and I have lived it from the very start. Like a magnetic force field on metal shavings, this mono-myth has constellated my thoughts, my strivings, and my life into a long odyssey of homecoming. I would say that I am presently taking my oar on the inner journey.

Growth Questions

1 Where is the divine in your journey? Where do you sense
   its influence or activity? How has this mythic form been
   the story of your life as well?

2 Do you hear the subtle voice of the inner divine feminine
   whispering guidance to you? This is your own intuition.
   Do you trust it? Do you listen? Can you explore the possibility that you are already somehow divine?

3 If this were Heaven on Earth right where you are, how
   would you live your life differently? How would you feel?

Chapter 9

Men Mentoring Men: Turning Growth into New Life

You and I are Odysseus wending our way home, but too often we travel alone. Why not join forces and travel the many lands of *The Odyssey* together? Who else can know what it is to grieve our wounds, amend our mistakes, sacrifice the warrior, come home to love, awaken our own wisdom and spirituality, and turn this growth into new life? For me, the best way to achieve these ends is through older men's mentoring groups.

Dictionaries define a mentor as one who offers sage advice or counsel to a younger person. In fact, the word comes from the role Mentor played in *The Odyssey*. As you will recall, Odysseus asked both Mentor and Eumaios, the swineherd, to look after his palace and his son while he was away at war. The latter becomes a kindly father substitute for Telemachus. Mentor, on the other hand, becomes something more. Through the influence of Athena, who repeatedly assumes his form, he serves as caring teacher, tutor, advisor, and supporter for Telemachus. It is the feminine spirit moving into the substitute father figure that stirs the young man's capacity for personal vision, risk-taking, and growth.

While the role of a male mentor usually involves the relationship between an older and a younger man, it seems to me that it could just as appropriately refer to older men helping each other. Thus was born the idea of the *male mentoring group*. Its goals include helping each other cope with the stresses and losses of aging, understanding and embracing the growth challenges in this time of life, digging deeper to find the unique soul work each man longs for, and providing support and encouragement to take new risks in love and work.

Ideas for starting and running an Older Men's Mentoring Group can be found in the Appendix. Once men form such a group, it is helpful to anticipate the issues that will more than likely arise.

The Issues of Aging Men

Over the course of writing this book, I led a men's gathering on aging, facilitated numerous ongoing male mentoring groups, met with a group of bright and capable octogenarians, and had discussions with forty men between the ages of 60 and 85. The men I met in these venues all had fairly successful careers, many in the helping professions, and many of them I had known for years. Our long-term friendships allowed our conversations to go deeper faster than would normally be the case. I am certain, however, that the aging themes these men expressed are universal. In other words, I believe that *these men discussed issues that all men face though not all men will talk about.*

My conversations with these men were rich, deep and poignant, resonating easily with my own experience. And as we shared, we grew. I have always understood that anything we feel, no matter how difficult, will evolve and transform when shared with another, and this was equally true with these men. Our worst fears, deepest disappointments, or greatest regrets softened and changed as we shared them. We also found common ground in the expression of the same universal themes. I am grateful to these men who generously gave so much to my experience of aging.

To help you connect with these men, I share some common beginning and emerging themes characterizing their group experience. These themes are not meant as prescriptions, and not every one voiced them all, but as recurring motifs they brought men together and felt familiar to most. I also presented my interpretation of *The Odyssey* to several men's groups as I wrote this book, inviting their insights and reactions. As we shared our impressions, our understanding of the story and each other deepened and I came to feel that *The Odyssey* could be of tremendous value for an older men's mentoring group.

Beginning Themes

War Fatigue. From the moment older men begin to understand their lives through the metaphor of war, they talk of war fatigue. Like Odysseus, they are tired of the competition, the daily grind, and the disconnection from their evolving self. They want more time for family, personal growth, exercise, interests, and the sharing of their gifts and experiences with others. They long to shift from tired warrior to energized elder but often don't know how to make this happen.

Anxiety about Retirement. For many men, the prospect of retirement triggers significant, albeit unspoken, anxiety, and those who do retire often rush immediately into hobbies, part-time jobs, and volunteer work to keep from experiencing it. They strive to keep their anxiety in abeyance with psychological defenses like suppression ("I don't think about it"), denial ("Retirement won't be hard for me at all"), happy fantasies ("I'm certain my retirement will be completely satisfying"), and compulsive activity ("I'm too busy to retire"). Once retired, they often have difficulty structuring their days productively, either doing too much as if still on-the-job or occupying their time with computer activities, TV, chores or exercise regimes – does this remind you of Odysseus's early mistakes? With probing, some men will acknowledge fear that the unstructured space of retirement may release emotional issues from the past, including depression, substance abuse, or marital conflict. They also fear that retirement itself may symbolize and even hasten death.

Feelings of Insignificance after Retirement. Older men, especially those who have retired, frequently complain about the loss of their occupational status, authority, and place in the world, and struggle with feelings of invisibility and insignificance. "What good am I now?" is a common refrain. Accustomed to position, respect, and productivity, they have no important identity to buttress their self-worth. A lifetime of meaning, achievement, and significance can disappear overnight. Men also mourn the loss of their parenting roles. With adult children now in their own lives, they feel forgotten or marginalized.

Loneliness. Another common theme is the absence of other men willing to talk honestly about the issues of aging. Most men find social connections through work and parenting – and eventually lose both supportive contexts in the aging process. Many describe approaching senior service groups or associations, or starting spontaneous conversations with other older men, only to find conversations limited to old "war stories", repetitive jokes, sports headlines, or political opinions. In the face of personal comments, the conversations faltered abruptly. Though surrounded by people, inside men feel lonely for real friends with whom they can discuss their deeper concerns and struggles of the heart.

The Pain of Loss. Most men identify significant recent or impending losses. One man's sister and another man's wife were dying of cancer, another's sister died recently, nearly all had lost one or both parents, and some had already lost friends, siblings, or children. They also talked about the pain of losing their career and sense of purpose, and struggled with finding meaningful substitutes. Not surprisingly, times of depression attend these physical, occupational. and social losses, but it is a muted depression, stoically tolerated and rarely expressed. Some feel that they should take care of it by themselves, others that it represents a personal failing or abnormality. Few are able to express their sadness.

Concerns about Physical Decline. In the beginning, many men acknowledge feeling shame and embarrassment at the physical changes they are experiencing. Age-related physical limitations caused by arthritis, back or knee injuries, or other problems, along with generalized muscle loss, now compromise their strength and dexterity. One man described being unable to fight back during a home invasion robbery; another about lacking the flexibility to work on his favorite hobby restoring old cars; a third about making mistakes in home repairs, a fourth about giving up flying because he no longer trusts his skills. Diminished sensory functions, particularly hearing loss, further contribute to this feeling of declining powers. Naturally men also fear that this decline will only accelerate, become unbearable, and lead to death.

Concerns about Death. Nearly all men struggle with the realization that time is running out and many turn instinctively to friends and family for comfort. In the men's gathering on aging, I asked how many in the audience think frequently about death and nearly every hand went up. We all know death is coming but few want to talk about it and even fewer family members want to hear our fears. Men often turn to common psychological defenses such as "planning" to suicide if the quality of life ever becomes intolerable, but even those with the most serious intentions discover they do not want to die even when faced with terminal illness.

Financial Worries. Most men find discussing their personal finances to be especially uncomfortable, raising issues of comparative personal worth and career success. Many, however, will eventually admit to worrying about whether they have enough savings to meet their long-term needs especially in the face of catastrophic health declines. As money often represents self-respect, independence, and long-term security, its absence can be deeply demoralizing and few wish to be financially dependent on their families.

Happiness. Despite these hardships, most men also express positive feelings about aging. They value the freedom from work, social expectations, and personal responsibilities. In fact, many said these years constituted some of the happiest times in their life, especially when loss and loneliness are not overwhelming, when everyday activities feel purposeful and reinforcing.

New Family Relationships. A particularly bright spot for many is the arrival of grandchildren, providing highly satisfying and reinforcing new relationships. Young children love doting grandparents and both love the reciprocal attention, at least until grandchildren reach adolescence when peers and social activities can take precedence. At a time when a man's grown children are too busy to be engaged, grandchildren fill the void and provide a wonderful sense of purpose. Relationships with grandchildren also bring men back into their families with new roles – baby sitting, playing, reading stories, playing catch, going on vacation, and cheering at soccer games.

Unfinished Business. As aging proceeds, men realize that there is much unresolved in their lives, including old or new conflicts with adult children, regrets about their past behavior or relation-ships, and longing to contribute to family or community. Aging men want to give their lives to love though they struggle to know how best to express it and how to heal hurts left over from the past.

Longing to Contribute as Elders. While many hear about becoming "elders", few men feel they have really acquired that social status, understand what is involved, or know how to achieve it. Some older men acknowledge a deep yearning to fill the role of elder and wonder what kind of process or ritual might effect this transformation. They still want their lives to matter and helping others can represent particularly meaningful goals.

Spirituality. Some elders become more spiritual or religious with age, though this development usually represents the natural progression of an already existing interest. Still, spirituality and religion can become increasing meaningful and helpful as health changes and losses mount. Ultimate questions eventually arise - "Have I lived a good life?" "Does God exist?" "What about Heaven, Hell and judgment?"). For who is truly confident in their knowledge of what happens after death?

Given the realities of aging – loss of identity and social connections in retirement, declining relationships with adult children, tightening budgets, emerging physical decline, the inevitability of losing others, and the approach of death, these themes are hardly surprising. But they also drive the restlessness that can begin the journey of growth. Though men may know there is more to do, they may not know what that entails. What is most surprising and discouraging, however, is how infrequently men discuss these themes in everyday conversations. There is often a "disconnect" between experience and communication – some do not know how they feel; others maintain the warrior model of manhood that discourages the expression of vulnerability and emotion; and many simply have had little practice with opening their inner lives to others. Mentoring groups bridge this chasm, creating a safe context for identifying and sharing these themes.

Age, too, is an important factor. Men in their early sixties and still actively employed spend little time dwelling on themes of aging and decline; in fact, they are largely unable to relate to them at all. By seventy, and certainly after retirement or a major health crisis, most men can begin to identify these themes and, with support, appreciate the opportunity to discuss them. As men move into their late seventies and eighties, as their world steadily shrinks, they turn increasingly to a handful of friends and family members for comfort and security, and to simpler ways of contributing to others, such as small acts of kindness and validation of others' worth, and to the inner task of preparing for death.

Emergent Themes

As the men open up and share their lives, new themes emerge, including:

Relief. Men often feel incredibly relieved to finally be giving voice to all they have locked up inside – relieved to know that what they feel is normal, understandable, and even growth-producing. They are relieved to no longer have to carry these issues alone. Relief lifts the burden of solitary sorrow. They are also relieved to know that they are now on a meaningful journey. As a result, their lives and thoughts become more focused, more directed toward the work of personal growth.

New Hope. Instead of feeling helpless in the face of seemingly insurmountable problems, men begin to realize there is much they can do to cope with aging. Some problems can be broken down into manageable pieces and actually solved, some simply become less distressing once feelings and concerns are shared, and the unfixable "big ones" can be gradually accepted because they represent the common destiny of all men and the group can support each member as he passes through them. Whatever is going to happen, group members feel they will not be alone, abandoned, or forgotten.

Pleasure in Being Together. Once real sharing has begun, men begin to look forward to their time in a group. It's fun, it's enlivening, and its real connection that grows by the week. Laughter, jokes, nicknames, references to past topics and stories weave a culture of male friendship that many say has been missing in their lives for too long. Having found it again, few things are more important than their group. They celebrate like the Phaeacians celebrated Odysseus.

Knowing Each Other More Deeply. With time and sharing, men come to know each other as brothers and family. They work on each member's concerns and problems. Rather than replacing their existing families, these new relationships release the energies of love, so that spending time with existing families is more fun, gratifying, and meaningful. Life feels more vivid, vital, and alive. In fact, they value simply "checking in" each session and catching up with the adventures, crises, and loves of each man.

Taking Meaningful Action in the World. When men move through *The Odyssey*, they observe over and over again how Odysseus keeps returning to his warrior ways, and how tired they are of that motif in our culture. They notice the countless ways that government and culture fail women, the young, the poor, the immigrants and the old, and they want to help somehow. This desire to make a difference marks the beginning of elder consciousness. With guidance and support, men begin to explore their own gifts and resources, and help each other imagine concrete ways to act constructively in the world, ways that come not from the head or the old workaholic compulsivity but from the heart and from a man's own nature. It need not be big; it just needs to be meaningful. In this way, a men's mentoring group can become a council of elders stepping into the rightful places in the community.

Taking Care of Others. Invariably men need to take care of each other and their families – being there for a loved one coming out of surgery, caring for a wife in the throes of serious illness, or helping a grandchild with a developmental disability. In the past, such tasks might have seemed daunting, threatening, or undesirable, but now we realize that our work is love and these challenges ask us to open that gift. With the support of other men, these tasks become profound and unbelievably important – every event a threshold in the journey home.

Becoming Who You Really Are. Over the months and years, as men experience the joy and importance of being seen and known by real friends, a feeling grows that you are finally becoming who you really are. No more games, pretenses, or hesitations. It's time to give yourself the greatest gift of all – acceptance.

Transcending Your Story. Telling his story in a group allows a man to work through leftover regrets, defeats, and mistakes, and then let them go. One man wrote a very poignant autobiography and self-published it. He was surprised to realize that this act also helped him transcend his story – it was in the book, not in him any more, and he was free to move on no longer bound by its struggles.

Facing the Reality of Death. Just like Odysseus, each man will face his own death. In the past, men dealt with that fear through stoic denial. In a men's group, we begin to wonder out loud, "What will death be like?" "Who do I want to be with me?" "How can we help each other?" Knowing that you will not die alone is so important. In some groups, men make the ultimate commitment – to be there for each man when the time comes. Men also find that they need to talk to their children about these concerns and encourage each other to do so. One 79-year-old man described a discussion with his adult children about where to spread his ashes. He had given his daughter thirty redwood trees to plant on her farm for her thirtieth birthday some years ago. She immediately knew that she wanted his ashes in this maturing grove. With this kind of reassurance, men put their death questions aside and turn to life instead, free to risk all in the service of love.

Transformation. Sharing, growing, and loving all lead to real life change. We are changed in this kind of group. We become better people, more capable of love, wisdom, and action. Men looking back on their group experiences nearly always comment on how much the group changed them from isolated, confused, depressed old guys making all the common mistakes of aging to men with purpose and love. This change is nothing short of transformation.

Beyond these beginning and emerging themes lie horizons that we must find through experience. They may involve new insights, work, or spiritual transformations. The excitement, however, resides in not knowing, sharing them with your best friends, and feeling the return of passion.

Growth Questions

1 Do you feel a need for mentoring from other men? Do you wish you could be in a group like the ones described? What stops you from finding or starting one?

2 What Beginning Themes most reflect your feelings about aging? Can you describe them in your own words? Which Emerging Themes would you most wish to experience? Why?

3 What kind of work do you long for most in these years? Create a vision of doing something new filled with inspiration, passion, and creativity. What does your vision look like?

Chapter 10

Rekindling Passion

Older men need to feel productive. They want to matter and contribute meaningfully to the world. They are not "done" and feel passionate about "giving back" or "making a difference". But finding a truly satisfying way to contribute is neither simple nor obvious and men often try out several possibilities without success, sometimes becoming discouraged and self-critical in the process. It is not just about having a job, it's about making the world a better place. If your customary work continues to be truly exciting, by all means continue. But if you secretly feel bored, restless, and used up in this endeavor, consider rekindling your passion either outside of work or in place of it.

Common paths for rekindling passion include mentoring younger men and volunteer work. Older men love to share their experience and expertise with younger people. Sadly, many younger people won't ask, feeling self-conscious, embarrassed or undeserving, or they are simply too busy to make time for mentoring. If you want to pursue a mentoring relationship, identify someone you would like to assist and become their friend. Don't mention mentoring itself - it sounds too formal or may imply criticism. Instead let mentoring develop naturally in the context of a friendly and trusting relationship. Ask questions, show interest, have coffee together with no agenda. Mentoring will happen by itself as each of you open up.

While helping others through volunteer work can feel good, often replacing the sense of community and social reinforcement previously found in employment, it may not bring the meaning and excitement we long for. Certainly it's good to have someplace to go, new friends, and new challenges and goals, and if volunteer work meets your needs for meaning and passion, then you are on your path. But this option does not meet every man's need for rekindled passion. Some men sense they have something deeper to give the world.

Searching for the Scent of Excitement

How do we find a meaningful and passionate focus for our creative energies in later years? What activity is worth getting up for every day and how do you find it? Consider these guidelines.

Don't accept the easy answers of volunteer work, part-time jobs, second careers, or exercise unless they truly excite you. Explore them, sample them, but don't make hasty commitments. Finding your passion not only takes time, it takes an inner search until the doorway of excitement opens again. And even when you are discouraged, don't give up. The search itself is part of your journey.

Look for your passion in who you are and what you do most naturally. Our gifts dwell in our very nature, our core basic personality. It's what we do when we have nothing to do, or the interests and activities that spontaneously draw our attention when we have free time. Because we take them for granted, the most obvious gifts are the easiest to miss or dismiss.

Your gift may be mirrored in the people you admire most. Make a list of your heroes. Don't dampen your enthusiasm with "realistic" considerations ("Oh I couldn't be like him!"). You won't be your hero, but you will be your version of what he represents. One man was drawn to the philosophy of Martin Luther King; he read about his life, and began to write letters and opinion pieces to newspapers giving voice to his deep passion for social justice. What would your hero want you to do?

Another approach is to ask others to list and describe your gifts. See which observations, traits, and behaviors keep recurring in their descriptions. Don't dismiss their observations in modesty; accept and look for the truth in them. Similarly, try to remember earlier times in your life when you felt excited just to be alive. Where were you? What were you doing? Why were you so motivated?

When exploring new directions or dreams, play the children's game of "hot and cold". List as many as you can and go down the list, sensing how "hot" (exciting) or "cold" (unexciting) each item feels. Whether an item is realistic, practical, or even possible is not important; you need to be completely free of judgment or analysis to follow the scent of excitement. The hallmarks of real passion are spontaneous excitement, a groundswell of motivation, genuine happiness, sudden creative urges, and more authentic and loving relationships. It usually starts with excitement.

Make a list next of all the obstacles to your dreams. Put in everything you can think of – lack of money, fear of failure, self-doubt, wasting time, disapproval from others, your age, and so forth. Then put the list aside and start to follow your dream with "baby steps". Avoid big decisions but make subtle movement in the "hot" direction – at the very least you'll be happier! Set aside time each week to have fun with your passion. Like courting a girl, flirt with this new love, spend time with it, and get to know it. Reach out to others expressing the same passion and share your interests. Resist setting goals or being practical – it doesn't have to make sense, just do it. Where you find the scent of excitement, you will find the path.

Passionate Motivation

When you do what you love, what you are made and meant to do, the journey seems to progress by itself. I know a man who loves the outdoors – nature, river rafting, and hiking. It has always been his passion, he just never had enough time for it. Upon retiring, he wanted to do something meaningful and important. As a physician, he thought he should offer his knowledge to free clinics or disadvantaged youth. He certainly had a lot to offer but just couldn't make himself pursue this path

– it felt too much like the work he left. Playing outdoors, on the other hand, felt selfish and hedonistic. Ignoring his doubts, I encouraged him to do what he loved.

After overcoming his resistance, Tim began to cycle. He took long trips up the river bike trail loving the sunshine and physical exertion. He began riding with a friend and they brought another friend. Then one day, he thought he'd join a biking fundraiser for multiple sclerosis. It was fun and productive so he did several more fundraisers. He was getting closer to his passion, but not quite on target. Then he initiated his own fundraiser to support a free clinic in his neighborhood. He started small, just did it and gave the money to the clinic. They were thrilled, interest grew, and soon he had quite a following. Others wanted to help and all loved the rides. None of this was planned. It just came from the path of passion. What will come next is anyone's guess, but as surely as water carries boats, this man's passion will carry him onward. There is no "goal" to be reached – but you will get "there" with passion.

The Surprises of Passion

Don, a retired minister, headed a national religious organization. Busy, important, and creative, he led the organization with energy and vision. Two bouts with cancer, however, began to change him. While he kept pursuing this second career, something was missing in his heart. One day, taking his grand-daughter to a summer horse-riding day camp, he fell in love with a brand new filly. He began visiting her every day. Soon he took lessons in horse training. He could not explain this new passion nor could he forget it. Something entirely new and unexpected was happening. Fortunately, Don did not question his excitement. This baby horse was giving him back his life.

I suspect Don's new passion will be a springboard to even more contact with nature. He finds himself wanting to spend more time with his roses. There is something in nature that calls to him. He says that he wants to meet the natural world on its terms, which is why horse-training is so interesting to him. You don't just train a horse, you learn its language – what the position of the ears means, how to approach a horse without being threatening, how to predict its behavior. For Don, meeting the world on its terms means developing a new and receptive relationship with reality – one that reveals a path into the enchantment of life. Where this passion will lead is unknown but the moral is clear: Do look a gift horse in the mouth, let her into your heart, and see where the two of you travel together.

The Gifts of Passion

Odysseus' passion was to come home. He didn't pursue another passion after that probably because neither Homer nor his culture had much experience with this "Third Age". We are the pioneers now. It is up to us to ignite and follow the passions that will transform our lives and western culture. This transformation comes from the many gifts of passion, including:

New Vision. When we find our passion, our vision of the world changes as if we had dropped our habitual blinders and suddenly see everything in a new way, in a new light. Instead of boredom, problems, or obstacles, we discover possibilities. Like buying a new tool, we search for ways we want to use it.

New Meaning, Purpose and Creativity. With passion, life fills with meaning and purpose again. We can't wait for the next chance to pursue what we love. Like riding a raft through the whitewater, we jump on and see where the current will take us. Even more amazing is the realization that we are the current now – we are riding our unfolding nature.

New Energy. By its very definition, passion is energy and when we tap into it, we are empowered. Like the cycling physician or the minister and his frisky filly, passion bursts with energy. We don't even have to be physically fit, for this energy can flow through so many different channels – art, poetry, computers, conversations, and projects.

New Connections. Vision, meaning, purpose, creativity, and energy drive us into the world now, bringing us into new friendships, adventures, and places. We make connections to others who share our excitement, forging new relationships in the world. We build bridges to people and places we might never have expected as if guided by unseen hands. Perhaps we are.

New World. Not surprisingly, in the flow of passion we rediscover the world around us – new friends, places, associations, ideas, and travel. Rather than drying up like old leaves, we are vital again. Our life renews all by itself. Then, in touch with our inner feminine, we fall in love with the world.

New Whole. Around the time *The Odyssey* was written, another Greek was describing the universal mystical experience of the unity. Hippocrates said, "There is one common flow, one common breathing. All things are in sympathy." When we find our passion, we become part of that whole in sympathy with all of it. Like a puzzle piece, we know where we fit and why. We finally understand our reason for living.

Passion builds the framework for this new stage of life. Like planting a new ground cover, it spreads everywhere and soon the hillside is abloom. We don't ask questions, we just follow the path of passion. Eventually, as the body ages and the fires of passion retreat into smoldering coals, we settle down but know that we have completed the work we came to do.

Growth Questions

When were you most passionate and excited about life? Recall the context, activities, and energy of that time. What made it so exciting?

Make your list of potential new activities for your life. When you're done, put a hot or cold rating by each item. You might even rate each on a 10-point scale from most to least hot or cold. What are you discovering?

Start small. Start today. Do something that brings the scent of excitement. Feel the energy. Keep coming back to it during the week. Like a beagle on the scent of a fox, follow your excitement on this new path. Where is it getting hotter, where is it colder? Let this exploration be fun.

Chapter 11

So What Do Aging Men Really Want?

From Odysseus, and from the many men who shared their lives with me, I believe that these are the fervent desires of aging men:

We want to leave the war. We are tired of the war. We are tired of fighting. We are not even sure what we are fighting for any more. This is not the way we want to live.

We want to come home to love. We traveled far out into the world as men and now, in aging, we want to come home again, like Odysseus, to family, friends, community, and love.

We want to help. Knowing now what the journey took, how demanding and challenging it was, how much we had to overcome, and how great were the joy and the pain, we long to help others on the path - children, grandchildren, friends old and new - to reach their goals and, one day, to find their way home, too.

We want to share our lives with others. We want to tell our stories and offer our wisdom, humor, and experience for the sheer joy of sharing this great adventure of life. Having experienced so many eras, events, people, and places, we are living museums of history. Take a tour through our memories.

We want forgiveness. We know we were selfish, self-centered, and even stupid at times, and deeply regret the pain we caused. Can you forgive us? Can we forgive ourselves?

We want to matter. We want to be needed and included, not just looked after. We have so much to offer and we know that others still need our love, gifts and guidance.

We want to stay involved. Our love for family, friends, sports, politics, music, news, history, science, travel, and culture still enrich our lives, and we do not intend to drop out.

We want passion-filled and meaningful work. We know our gifts are born from the passions still inside us and we want to express them. Work now is not about making money but about manifesting who we really are in the service of helping others.

We want to have fun. We want to laugh, dance, watch movies, go out for dinner, play with kids, attend concerts and sporting events - whatever we used to love, we may still or we'll find something new.

We want to be seen as unique individuals. We are not all alike, not cookie-cutter repetitions of the "old people" form. Nor are we a separate species. We have spent a lifetime individuating – we want to be seen for ourselves.

We want to keep learning. There are new things to learn and understand in each phase of life, and aging is no exception. Learning is not just filling time; it's growth, excitement, novelty, and preparation for our next challenge.

We want to find meaning. We want to apply the lessons of history, philosophy, religion, and science to our own lived experience. Reflecting on who we were and what we did, we want to find the meaning of our lives and times.

We want physical connection and experiences. Getting old doesn't mean giving up the body! Hugs, exercise, sports, and nature are as important as ever – though our activity level may be a little less vigorous. The need for touch in particular never ends - kids on our laps, embraces for greetings, playful contact, cuddling. We may still want to make love, just a little slower and with more sensuality.

We want to stay as independent as is reasonable. At each step of our changing health, we ask for freedom, choice, and self-determination. We don't want to be coddled or protected; we want honest, respectful and two-way conversation about real choices. Our freedom is the vehicle for the continued expression of self and love.

We want to prepare for death. Though it may be difficult and scary, we want to talk with family, friends, physicians, and clergy about what we need, how we feel, and even how they can support our passage from this world. We need to say goodbye and to die well.

We want to awaken a spiritual comprehension of life. We are approaching an amazing threshold, a passage through the veil. We sense this mystery though we're not sure what will happen. But if there was ever a time to open our spiritual eyes, it is now.

We want our culture to wake up from the incessant drumbeat of fear, competition and war. Fear messages are everywhere – "Danger!" "Child abductions!" "Terrorists!" "Weapons of mass destruction!" "Global warming!" "Plagues!" "Death panels!" "Be afraid!" "Be a warrior!" "Compete for survival!" Aging men see the tragic consequences of this war psychology everywhere and want it to stop before we have destroyed life on this planet.

Final questions
And with all this in mind, we ask ourselves some final questions.

- *Have I finally opened my heart to love, and loved as fully and deeply as possible?*
- *Have I given my gifts of self and soul to the world?*
- *Have I faced my wounds, forgiven others, and asked for others' forgiveness in turn?*
- *Am I taking care of my responsibilities to family, friends, and community?*
- *What practical actions – legal, financial, moral - do I still need to take?*
- *How am I emotionally preparing to die?*
- *What have I learned from this lifetime?*
- *What does the complete arc of a life look like?*

Our Last Wish

The Odyssey describes the possible cultural transition from warrior to friend, conqueror to lover, too-smart animal to awakened spiritual being – a journey that humanity is still very much in the process of taking together, an odyssey that is critical to our survival on this planet. Coming home to love, our last wish as mature elders is to serve this great transition. We are here to help and have much to offer. Let's do it together.

Growth Questions

1 Underline three of the above "wants" that most express your desires. Elaborate on them. Get in touch with your heart's longing. Let it move you toward the risk of change and growth.

2 Pick one of the seven Final Questions that holds meaning or energy for you and explore it further. Why did you pick that question? What is left to do on that theme?

3 How can you take a stand against war? How can you help guide the young and the leaders of this culture to peaceful and non-violent solutions to human conflict? How can you help change the war mentality of men?

Chapter 12

Poems for Aging Odysseans

I conclude this journey with two poems written for Odysseus. Read them slowly. Let them speak to your heart and guide your journey home. Their message is powerful: The journey is the goal, not the destination, so take your time, go deep, and understand the true meaning of home.

Ulysses
Lord Alfred Tennyson

It little profits that an idle king,
By this still hearth, among these barren crags,
Matched with an aged wife, I mete and dole
Unequal laws unto a savage race,
That hoard, and sleep, and feed, and know not me.
I cannot rest from travel; I will drink
life to the lees. All times I have enjoyed
Greatly, have suffered greatly, both with those
that loved me, and alone; on shore, and when
Through scudding drifts the rainy Hyades
Vexed the dim sea. I am become a name;
For always roaming with a hungry heart
Much have I seen and known—cities of men
And manners, climates, councils, governments,
Myself not least, but honored of them all—
And drunk delight of battle with my peers,
Far on the ringing plains of windy Troy.
I am part of all that I have met;
Yet all experience is an arch wherethrough
Gleams that untraveled world whose margin fades

Forever and forever when I move.
How dull it is to pause, to make an end.
To rust unburnished, not to shine in use!
As though to breathe were life! Life piled on life
Were all too little, and of one to me
Little remains; but every hour is saved
From that eternal silence, something more,
A bringer of new things; and vile it were
For some three suns to store and hoard myself,
And this gray spirit yearning in desire
To follow knowledge like a sinking star,
Beyond the utmost bound of human thought.

This is my son, my own Telemachus,
To whom I leave the scepter and the isle
Well-loved of me, discerning to fulfill
This labor, by slow prudence to make mild
A rugged people, and through soft degrees
Subdue them to the useful and the good.
Most blameless is he, centered in the sphere
Of common duties, decent not to fail
In offices of tenderness, and pay
Meet adoration to my household gods,
When I am gone. He works his work, I mine.
There lies the port; the vessel puffs her sail;
There gloom the dark, broad seas. My mariners,
Souls that have toiled, and wrought, and thought with me
That ever with a frolic welcome took
The thunder and the sunshine, and opposed
Free hearts, free foreheads—you and I are old;
Old age hath yet his honor and his toil.
Death closes all; but something ere the end,
Some work of noble note, may yet be done,
Not unbecoming men that strove with gods.

The lights begin to twinkle from the rocks;
The long day wanes; the slow moon climbs; the deep
Moans round with many voices. Come, my friends.
'Tis not too late to seek a newer world.
Push off, and sitting well in order smite
The sounding furrows; for my purpose holds
To sail beyond the sunset, and the baths
Of all the western stars, until I die.
It may be that the gulfs will wash us down;
It may be that we shall touch the Happy Isles,
And see the great Achilles, whom we knew.
Though much is taken, much abides; and though
We are not now that strength which in old days
Moved earth and heaven, that which we are, we are
One equal temper of heroic hearts,
Made weak by time and fate, but strong in will
To strive, to seek, to find, and not to yield.

Ithaka
C. P. Cavafy

As you set out for Ithaka
hope your road is a long one,
full of adventure, full of discovery.
Laistrygonians, Cyclops,
angry Poseidon—don't be afraid of them:
you'll never find things like that on your way
as long as you keep your thoughts raised high,
as long as a rare excitement
stirs your spirit and your body.
Laistrygonians, Cyclops,
wild Poseidon—you won't encounter them
unless you bring them along inside your soul,
unless your soul sets them up in front of you.

Hope your road is a long one.
May there be many summer mornings when
with what pleasure, what joy,
you enter harbors you're seeing for the first time;
may you stop at Phoenician trading stations
to buy fine things,
mother of pearl and coral, amber and ebony,
sensual perfume of every kind—
and may you visit many Egyptian cities
to learn and go on learning from their scholars.

Keep Ithaka always in your mind.
Arriving there is what you are destined for.
But don't hurry the journey at all.
Better if it lasts for years,
so you're old by the time you reach the island,
wealthy with all you've gained on the way,

not expecting Ithaka to make you rich.

Ithaka gave you the marvelous journey.
Without her you would not have set out.
She has nothing left to give you now.
And if you find her poor, Ithaka won't have fooled you.
Wise as you will have become, so full of experience,
you'll have understood by then what these Ithakas mean.

Growth Questions

1 What line, image or theme in each poem touches you most deeply? Why? What does it want from you?

2 Tennyson's last sentiment is so powerful. He seems to be saying that while we are not what we were, there is still another horizon to seek. What is that for you?

3 Cavafy tells us not to hurry this journey home, for the journey is the purpose. Can you see the wisdom in that advice? Can you value each day you are on this great road?

Starting an Older Men's Mentoring Group

To create and facilitate a male mentoring group, consider the following steps:

1 Interview older men likely to appreciate this vision of the journey of age. Form a group and make a commitment to support each other with sensitivity, caring, and honesty. Agree to meet weekly if possible for an hour and a half.

2 Get to know each other more deeply by telling your individual life stories, one man per session. Honor each man's life with understanding and compassion.

3 Once every man has told his story, begin to read *The Odyssey* using the original text or my distillation. Explore the eighteen challenges (or twenty) described, focusing on one per session. Read the challenges between sessions and ask each man to be prepared to discuss the detail that touched him most, identify how he experienced that symbolic challenge in his actual life, and answer the growth questions at the end of the chapter. Take your time and be sure everyone participates. (If you are reading the full text, remember that Homer began describing the challenges in the middle so proceed in this order: Books IX, X, XI, XII, V, VI, VII, VIII, and XIII-XXIV).

4 Along the way, always make space for any one who needs more time or is currently experiencing more acute distress around one of these challenges in his life. Generally speaking, the deeper you go in a safe and supportive context, the more you will grow.

5 After completing the story, consider creating an initiation ritual for each man (see guidelines in the Appendix). Make

it as large or intimate as you want as long as it feels sincere and meaningful. Let each person decide when he is ready for this initiation. You may discover that men do not feel ready for initiation until they have reached at least 65 or 70 years of age.

6　If possible, continue meeting indefinitely because the challenges tend to recycle and we need to mentor each other over and over again.

7　One last piece of advice: Stay in the here and now, not in your head. Intellectual debate of politics, religion, or the world deadens a group's vitality, as do discussions of sports, current events, philosophy, and other heady topics. If the group is having difficulty staying with self-disclosure, feelings, and personal matters, find a therapist or related professional to facilitate the group. Similarly signs of a dying group include members missing sessions, arriving late or leaving early, or avoiding authentic sharing.

Ritual for an Elder's Initiation

Below are ideas for two kinds of elder rituals, the first blending initiation with retirement, birthday, or moving parties, and the second involving a more formal ceremony.

Blending Initiation with Elder Celebrations

Any celebration for an elder, including retirement, birthdays and moving parties, can be turned into a meaningful initiation ritual by including these elements:

- Invite everyone he loves.
- Bring thoughtful cards, gifts, art, or home made presents.
- Consider a toast, roast, song, poem, or skit for the occasion.
- Make his special meal and dessert.
- Share memories and photographs of his life.
- Ask about the elder's hopes, dreams, and goals for the future.
- Give voice to participants' hopes, dreams, and wishes for the elder's new life.
- Have fun, take your time, and laugh.

Through these acts, we mark and celebrate an elder's passage in a way that validates his life, gives permission for him to let go of the past, and creates a new vision for his future. Though such a celebration may seem trivial on the surface, it embellishes common secular gatherings with the implicit symbolic and mythic significance of initiation.

Planning a Formal Elder Ritual

An elder initiation can also be done formally, creating a powerful and transformational ceremony. A formal ritual commonly comprises four elements and four stages. Using this model, planners build a social event with amazing results.

Four Basic Elements. The basic elements of an elder ritual consist of community support and preparation, ritual context, sacred encounter, and integration.

Community Support and Preparation. Initiation cannot be performed alone. It requires the involvement of others (or as many as are personally relevant to the initiate) to share in its conception and preparation, and to witness and embrace the transformed elder's vision.

Ritual Context. Invoking the sacred in accordance with one's religious or spiritual beliefs is the heart of ritual. Initiation needs to be understood as a sacred act to be performed in a sacred context. Creating a ritual context may be as simple as beginning with a prayer or meditation, or as complex as the one described below. It also includes a beginning process of purification that sets the stage for entering sacred space, a middle phase in which the sacred is encountered in some way, and an ending that closes the space and assimilates its revelations.

Sacred Encounter. An initiate needs some kind of first hand experience of the sacred to sanctify his struggle and provide a new life vision. In sacred space, he seeks divine guidance and revelation, and recognizes divinity's "response" which constitutes a grace that completely transcends the ego's abilities and agenda. The initiate's sincerity, spiritual understanding and preparation, and depth of longing are also critical to the success of the encounter.

Integration. Whatever transpires in this sacred encounter must be assimilated into the elder's personal values, identity, and place in the community. The integration process extends beyond the ceremony, takes time and periodic review.

Four Stages of Initiation. The elder's initiation consists of four stages: celebrating the past, dying to the past, entering sacred space, and returning to the world as an enlightened elder.

Celebrating the Past. An elder ritual summarizes, blesses, and celebrates the past, recalling who the elder has been and what he has accomplished. When this celebration is done with sincerity, sensitivity, and gratitude, the elder feels fully seen and acknowledged and can more readily retire outworn roles, duties, and identities in preparation for new ones.

Dying to the Past. Initiation revolves around the theme of death and rebirth - the death of an old life and the birth of a new one. An elder ritual provides an opportunity to say goodbye to the past and grieve all that the elder has left behind. It may also involve asking forgiveness from those who have been hurt and forgiving those who have hurt the elder in turn. Grief and forgiveness are part of the emotional work of letting go and moving on.

Entering Sacred Space. Remembering is not enough; transformation also requires an experience in sacred space. Rituals open this space, bringing together time and eternity, self and Self, if just for a moment. Sacred space is especially important for the elder who is approaching the border between this world and the next. Initiation invites the elder to enter sacred space and experience whatever insights, realizations, or experiences arise in it. It may, therefore, include a spiritual and religious practice such as silence, Presence, prayer, acts of purification, and blessing.

Returning to the World as an Enlightened Elder. Entering the sacred transfigures our experience of self, life and world. Initiation encourages an enlightened perception of the world and one's place in it. As a result, the world becomes a magical place of beauty, enchantment, and love. Service arises spontaneously from the joy of this experience expressed through new social roles (e.g., grandparent, historian, social conscience, activist, gardener, mentor, artist, and volunteer).

Building a Specific Ritual. Employing the four basic elements and four stages of initiation, planners create a ritual tailored to the elder's needs. The ritual includes specific assignments for both the planners and the elder.

The Planners' Assignment. Select a planning committee. Obtain authorization from the elder-to-be to plan their ritual and make a list of the most important attendees (e.g., friends, children, coworkers, relatives). Keep a manageable limit on the number of guests. Contact the attendees, explain the purpose of the gathering, elicit their cooperation, and select a date.

The planning committee meets several times before the initiation to reflect on the elder's life and create the most appropriate ritual. The following steps are suggested:

1 Planners are encouraged to consider questions like: Who has this person been in our life? What has he or she done? What is the essence of their contribution to others? What hardship or suffering in life revealed the gifts of character this individual brought into the world? What philosophy, values, or ultimate meaning subsequently guided this person's life? What roles, duties, and identities are over now?

2 Planners interview the elder around these same themes to help him or her prepare for the event and to ensure that the

planners really understand the person's life. They also ask about his spiritual beliefs, previous experiences with the divine, and what sacred space means to him.

3   Collect any pertinent physical memorabilia associated with this person's journey, including pictures, uniforms, diplomas, awards, music, and work products.

4   Planners prepare a short but rich summary of this material to be read aloud during the ritual so all understand the elder's life better.

5   Find or create a physical symbol that marks the elder's new life (e.g., article of clothing, ceremonial staff, poem or painting, etc). Be creative.

6   All attendees are asked to prepare remarks on what the elder has meant to them and bring a small symbolic gift (e.g., a poem, song, skit, artwork, or object).

7   The planning committee chooses a master of ceremonies to guide the ritual or divides ritual steps between them.

Elder's Assignment. The elder might be given instructions such as the following:

1   Reflect on your old life with these questions: Who have I been? What have I done? What has my life meant to me? How did suffering or hardship shape my character and reveal something of the gifts I was given to bring into the world? What philosophy, values, or ultimate meaning subsequently guided my life? What have I contributed to others? What roles, duties, or identities are over now? Who and what have I lost along the way? Which goodbyes were the most painful? What regrets do I have about my life? Who did I help and who did I hurt? Whose forgiveness do I need and who do I need to forgive? What is my relationship with the sacred? What is my way of loving the world and how might I express it in my new

life?

2 List the ancestors whose spirits you would most like to invite to your ritual (deceased parents, siblings, grandparents, and others as far back as you wish).

3 Prepare a few paragraphs summarizing the above reflections to be read aloud at the ritual.

4 You may also wish to prepare a poem, song, skit, or artwork symbolizing the meaning of this passage to be performed during the ritual. Also create a physical symbol of your old life.

5 Finally spend time in whatever way deepens your experience of the sacred (e.g., prayer, solitude, scripture, or spiritual practice). If this is difficult, consider some form of spiritual consultation or direction.

The Ritual. The actual ritual might involve a variation of these steps uniquely tailored to the community and the elder:

1 Arrive on time at the assigned gathering place. Stand or sit in a circle. Costumes, face painting, or drumming may be additional ritual elements. Avoid any small talk or trivial conversation that would diminish the sacred nature of this event. While the group reviews the ritual plan, the elder waits in another room and is instructed to quiet the mind and reflect simply on why he or she is here.

2 Mark the beginning of the ritual in some way (e.g., a bell, drum, formal announcement, music, or moment of silence) and then invite the elder to a special place on the circle. Participants remain in loving silence.

3 The master of ceremonies calls on the sacred and the elder's ancestors to be present in whatever way feels most meaningful and states the purpose of the ritual. The elder is asked to identify him or herself to the ancestors and the assembled group.

4 When steps one to three are completed, move through the following stages. The master of ceremonies (or selected others) explains and guides each step. Take whatever time is necessary - a ritual of this depth should not be rushed - and allow emotion to flow naturally when it comes up.

Leaving the Past: The planners discuss the elder's life, honoring him or her for how they have lived. Attendees then share what the elder has individually meant to them. Finally, the elder shares his or her own personal material about their life's meaning.

Grieving the Past: The elder is asked to talk about any sadness, grief, or regret they feel about the past, ask for whatever forgiveness is needed from anyone living or dead, and address anyone he or she needs to forgive. As a further symbol of this dark space, the lights may be turned off while the elder talks, leaving perhaps a single candle burning in the distance to symbolize the divine light of the next world. When completed, the elder may also be smudged with smoke to cleanse the past and purify the soul for entering sacred space, and the lights are turned back on.

Entering Sacred Space: A sacred space is physically marked on the floor in some way that divides the elder's old and new lives. The elder is asked to leave behind a physical symbol of his old life, step into sacred space, and state what it means to him. The participants are instructed to cease thinking, heighten awareness, and come into the divine presence and assembled ancestors however they conceive them. All remain in sacred space while the elder speaks publicly to the divine and the ancestors about his life. He also asks for guidance for his new life. Participants then do the same to the extent they are comfortable. In this sacred space the elder is also instructed to present whatever poem, song, skit, or artwork they have prepared followed by whatever the committee has prepared.

Returning to the World as an Enlightened Elder. The elder is instructed to step across the threshold from sacred space into the new world, experiencing him and the world itself as brand new. Encourage him to witness its beauty and perfection and praise all he sees. Finally the elder is asked to describe the various ways he or she wishes to serve this new world.

5   The elder is now welcomed into their new life and community with the physical symbol created by the planning committee along with song, praise, or hugs. The group remains in the circle imaging how the elder's potential gifts might be expressed in future roles. They comment on what the ritual revealed about the elder's essence and reason for being in the world? Symbolically meaningful presents are given during this sharing.

6   The ritual formally ends in the same way it began so that the sacred space of the initiation is closed. Gratitude is expressed to the divine and ancestors for their participation.

7   A mailing list of all in attendance is compiled and the elder promises to send a description of their life experience on the one-year anniversary of the ritual.

8   It is understood that the elder will now be available to help initiate other elders, forming a community of enlightened older people committed to mutual support in their new roles.

9   Refreshments are served and people stay until the event is over.

References

Cavafy, C. P. *Ithaka*. Retrieved 6/20/12 from http://www.cavafy.com/poems/content.asp?id=204&cat=1

Lattimore, Richmond. (1999). *The Odyssey of Homer*. New York: HarperPerennial.

Robinson, John. (1997). *Death of a Hero, Birth of the Soul*. Council Oaks Books.

Robinson, John. (2011). *Finding Heaven Here*. UK: John Hunt Publishing.

Robinson, John. (2012a). *The Three Secrets of Aging*. UK: John Hunt Publishing.

Robinson, John (2012b). *Bedtime Stories for Elders*. UK: John Hunt Publishing.

Tennyson, Alfred Lord. *Ulysses*. Retrieved 6/20/12 from http://www.portablepoetry.com/poems/alfredlord_tennyson/ulysses.html

Other Books by John Robinson

Death of a Hero, Birth of the Soul: Answering the Call of Midlife

But Where is God? Psychotherapy and the Religious Search

Ordinary Enlightenment: Experiencing God's Presence in Everyday Life

Finding Heaven Here

The Three Secrets of Aging

Bedtime Stories for Elders: What Fairy Tales Can Teach Us About the New Aging

Learn More at:
www.johnrobinson.org

**PSYCHE
BOOKS**

The study of the mind: interactions, behaviours, functions.
Developing and learning our understanding of self. Psyche
Books cover all aspects of psychology and matters relating to
the head.

9781780999814